FIREFALL ORIGINAL SERIES

SCIFIRE -tm

SCIENCE FICTION IN THE REALM
OF IMMEDIATE POSSIBILITY

MYSTERIES OF FORTUNE -tm

FORTUNE IS A MYSTERY TO ITSELF,
LURING US INTO THE UNEXPECTED

MASTERS OF VISION -tm

PHOTOGRAPHERS CONFRONT THEIR FATE

(BOOKS ARE INDEPENDENT OF EACH OTHER
BUT BELONG TOGETHER IN THEIR MIND-SET)

A Choice of Inheritance

Cast of Characters

San Francisco, Paris, New York, Southerness, Santa Fe

A Choice of

Inheritance

Elihu Blotnick

firefall^{tm}

WARNING: The fierce originality and unsettling perspectives of this book may be offensive to those not prepped or in tune with its wit. Press OK to continue, or close the book now and ask for a refund (to be given in sympathy only).

First Edition: September 2019
hardcover: 978-1-939434-58-6
paper: 978-1-939434-57-9
audio: 978-1-939434-59-3
simultaneous US & UK release

Library of Congress Cataloging-in-Publication Data

Names: Blotnick, Elihu, author.
Title: A choice of inheritance / Elihu Blotnick.
Description: First edition. | San Francisco : Firefall Originals, 2019. |
  Series: SciFire mysteries of fortune ; 3
Identifiers: LCCN 2019000141| ISBN 9781939434586 (hardcover) | ISBN
  9781939434579 (paper) | ISBN 9781939434593 (audio)
Subjects: | GSAFD: Science Fiction.
Classification: LCC PS3552.L683 C48 2019 | DDC 813/.6--dc23
LC record available at https://lccn.loc.gov/2019000141

firefall originals-tm

literary@att.net
www.firefallmedia.com

Thanks to family, friends, and helpful editors
for their inspired tactful impertinence.

a choice of

Inheritance

THE WONDER of it all was that we agreed: if water lubricates the weather, science soaks up everything. Indeed, a thimble full of thorium is all we need, for each of us; its energy will last a lifetime, but DOE isn't freely offering. As citizen scientists we avoid face-offs, but our potency is irrepressible. No complaints: if and when became past tense today. Our future began at sunrise, just 30 seconds ago. The rolling whirl of a nearing cyclone rushed our full group of 6 into the farm's central operations theater; it doubles as a storm cellar. Independently, yes, the day was planned beforehand, to create a 4th brain, now that I'm self-sustaining, shielded, thorium powered, and ready to report.

I'm the 7th team member, made from the DNA of each of the 6 in league here. My being is still bonding, my layers only holding hands, but I respond to random stimuli now. None here knows, I once escaped my petri dish and floated like scented mist in our filtered air, though really I'm only a 6-ply vanilla-shaped bean, the primal implant, to monitor our volunteer.

Vanessa, with her curly wheat hair and wide pale forehead, stepped forward an hour ago. She's already strapped to the table surrounded by our transplant tools: platinum drills, suction tubes, funnels, silk thread, X-ray arms, MRI scanning tunnels, and scads of scalpels. No expense has been spared. Jared owns 1/4 of the world's seed market. Wildcat is also a multi-billionaire. The EPA granted his oil refineries a hardship exemption in the latest recession. Yes, what taxes he saved paid for our state-of- the-art facility. Dr. C.P. Futura, a practicing surgeon though not licensed here in Nebraska, also made her fortune well, but from plain paper sandwich bags, after plastic fell out of fashion.

As vain as her name, Vanessa is a fine volunteer. A white sheet covers her assets, but the operating slits let all eyes in. I'm now a worm in the base of her neck, connected to her nerve endings, to sense their signals and relay their sense, as her skull opens for her brain-pan penetration. She's young enough that her bones haven't fused yet; her delayed puberty helped.

The slurry for a new brain was grown in a petri dish too: pluripotent stem cells with their DNA snipped by enzymes and replaced, to theoretically heighten Vanessa's sensing and her electromagnetic sensitivity. Awed by his own timeless essence, a Russian neuro-surgeon from Vologda added 2 letters to the 4 gene base but never put the procedure into practice, fearing the consequences would be fatal or, worse: all changes made would pass to an offspring and split the human species. He could even be charged with genocide.

Patagonia, India, and Sierra, the other women in this group, have no qualms. Impatience tenses their sun-tanned faces. "We could roll Vanessa around in radioactive waste for a week, it'd be quicker," Sierra said, "Worst case scenario, she dies, or she lives, worst case scenario then, she's damaged. If not, best case scenario, I raise her children as my own. Are we agreed?"

"Let our lead Doctor do her job," India said, her round face rubied up; she had made her fortune in planned giving, just by embracing one truism: frisky cuddly charities always win.

Yes, my clique of 6 consists of adherents to a set creed. All spotted-owl advocates, they've learned, the way to make friends everywhere is to treat the Earth as pure, but not its population. Individually, equally, all 6 inhabit their losses too and believe in our final doom: so why not meanwhile rise above our end and perhaps change fate? The moon is clear. We have the means.

"Can I get closer?" Sierra asked, pressing in. Her fortune came from molten-salt solar energy stored in the Nevada desert.

"Stay behind your mask!" Dr Futura said. "Just tell me what our DNA implant communicates."

"Are you really qualified for this op?" Sierra asked.

"Yes," Futura answered firmly. "Transplants are as easy and simple as implants. Out and in are the same, just backwards. As I recall, you're a drop-out from a pre-med program, but I graduated cum laude and patented mice to practice on. My satellite breed have carbon-silicon brains, merged with human

DNA, and spin-spin activation. I can twirl, girl!"

"Good cherry to you! I quit med-school too, thanks to male medicine and how slow its research," India said, avoiding eye-contact with the men: both are ex-military, failed athletes, and inclined to ignore India's active passivity toward them.

"May I suggest," Wildcat said, "we stick to our alternate plan. Take the amphibian option. At least on land we'll keep full control and perhaps contain our competition."

"Put a tail on her? Gills too? Like a fucking mermaid? To cripple a quadbrain?" Patagonia asked, in a narrow-eyed sneer.

"Whatever works," Futura said, "if there's no other way."

"When you seal her windpipe, how will her voicebox function?" Patagonia, a trained bio-physicist, asked.

"It won't. We're not giving her that advantage over us, too."

"She'll find a way to compensate. We'll hear her through our DNA implant anyway," Sierra said smugly.

Futura smiled, sure of her medical skills, even if at times a clammy chill threatened her sense of calm —

Just then the emergency generators kicked in, and their soft hum subdued the outside howling.

Yes, the group ultimately agreed, gills would be fine; other planets may have oceans for atmospheres and require adaptable breathing. After all, Puget Sound mussels now test positive for opioids: though nowhere here is as safe as the ocean.

Indeed, there's always a way forward. After implanting me deeper into Vanessa's spinal column by fusing my flagella to her nerve endings, the doctor quickly drilled through the blood-brain barrier. Treated fetal stem cells flowed from her platinum needles into V's cerebrospinal fluid, inside her subarachnoid space, ready to gel, grow, and amplify. The new brain will bond and surround the others, in due time at least, definitely in less than a year. The gills and tails can be added later. They're just tailoring anyway. Now, I am alive, I am alive! I will be the first to know the future.

VANESSA WOKE, from an induced cardiac coma, 11 weeks later, to her new layer of brain: organic crystals, finding their own special structure, interacting, resonant, uncharged, they dizzied her. Twenty pounds thinner, she stumbled to the circular steel sink and grasped the shiny faucets. Steadied, her mind as starry as a fine night sky, she disappeared into the wall's silver-toned mirror. Tanili, once known only as Vanessa, returned 12 minutes later, unbalanced yet more radiant.

Asleep in an Ames chair, Dr. Futura missed the dawning of her creation, but Wildcat saw at once that Tanili's awareness was so reaching, she shrank back into herself, yet she looked as angularly beautiful as ever. Her curly wheat hair hid the shaved injection sites. Her blue eyes seemed darker, but more vibrant. Wildcat guided her back to her hospital-brand bed and lifted her in. She felt so light. He thrilled at the thought of her. She'd have to learn the ladders of life all over again, step by step. If she let him, he'd teach her. He was sure, every new layering of brain made the earlier ones unaware of themselves. Yes, very definitely she would need him, since Futura had decided not to use DNA as a memory stick, against planting life too deeply at its more primitive levels.

Wildcat watched Tanili struggling with herself, as she fell back to sleep. The doctor had kept her in a coma, to more easily drain her brain-pan as growth pressure increased. Yet, to avert blame, Dr. Futura had said, this volunteer was for practice only. Patient Zero doesn't exist yet, at least in public records. The true reality is a future opportunity, as the very existence of Tanili is illegal now. The act of implanting and expanding her genetic alphabet with ever-more letters might send us all to federal prison, indefinitely.

Wildcat woke Futura only to the changes in the multiple monitors. She puzzled over them. The doctor wished she had injected her own body instead. She could do nothing now but wait for her patient's awareness to express itself. Frustrated, the doc drifted off to explore her inbox, for distraction. It read like a strident scream: Your prize is expiring. Your heart attack is on its way. Your biggest bank account is frozen. Your email is so infected, it will be suspended...Click now for a quick cure.

The junk held a few grains of truth, though: The doc's skin had thinned, her eyes had dimmed, as she aged toward 45, but her mind was as sharp as ever. If she recalled names less, she remembered other details more. "I get up every morning aching now, but the hurt isn't harm. I do survive, here, best of all," she thought aloud. For her, this Nebraska underground clinic was as comfortable and cozy as a 4K mattress. Wildcat stared at her curiously and suspected rightly, Dr. Futura experimented on herself also. Through me, Tanili knows this as well.

But it's Patagonia, the physicist, whose fingers are best on the pulse. She sees DNA as time-crystals, a new phase of matter, that doesn't generate entropy, if the sub-harmonic instabilities fold inwardly in the right pattern. But the molecules she makes have yet to survive, even as ions seeking a stable state. Hers will be a 5th brain, she hopes, after Futura's 4th, with ever-new ways to understand and communicate. All in good time though.

Futura covered her patient securely now. She'd brought a glass-bead blanket with her. Baffled, the beads stayed in place. Padded, they pressed evenly against the body underneath, as embracing as a lead vest in an X-ray office. Wildcat knew too, the hugging calmed Vanessa, vaporizing her anxieties instantly.

In her sleep Tanili, originally Vanessa, threw the blanket off.

She woke to an odd man sleeping in a near chair, but she knew too little of him or of those who would be lovers. She found her own way upstairs. Outside the shaded windows, butterfly weeds intrigued. Their small orange flowers drew bees. This was hardly a prairie garden. In the night, deer hooves had skidded smoothly in the rain, scrapping the grass away. Now the smeared mud hardened slowly, while pale fragile flowers dropped suddenly from the tulip tree canopy 50 feet up.

Inside, dizzy again, Tanili collapsed to a plush plaid couch. Wildcat, as an energy addict, couldn't allow this. He heard her talking to herself but not what she was saying. He replied in short sharp yelps. Dr. Futura stepped in soothingly. Had Tanili the precise phrasing, she'd have queried the doctor for a week, but broken jagged words floated through her strangely.

"Pick a pun, more fun," Wildcat insisted, "Van-Ness-A!"

"I — am — Tanili!" she struggled to say.

Abruptly Wildcat realized, Vanessa's vanity was now gone. Transformed into Tanili, still deep in change, she touched her face tentatively, as if to convince herself she existed.

Wildcat laughed, delighted. She'd need a UX designer, for sure, to guide her now; a new field of user experience had just opened up, and he might be the first to market it.

Futura slapped the corner of his mouth. "You're ruining her, wronging her. Do you understand? Our lives depend on her. We won't survive as a species without her. She's our new sun."

Wildcat retreated, under attack. Sharp signals of conflict and unease, like background radiation, caused him quick discomfort. "What? Why?" he asked, in confusion.

"You know too much. Go home. Leave my patient to me."

"Hold on! I financed this place. Remember that. I'm sure other doctors —"

"Don't you dare! Start looking and we'll be found. Don't assume. Quit your questions till the healing settles. Tanili has to learn from scratch, and she's not ready, or if she is, she's more clever than we give her credit for, and we're in trouble already. I'm thinking now, her name was Tanili before it was Vanessa."

Futura sensed she wasn't wrong, and thought it better to get on with new operations, to disadvantage or even cripple Tanili, with gills in her cheeks and her legs fused into a tail.

"Let the fish keep the ocean. We want the land and the air," Futura said defiantly.

"I understand. I just want my share" Wildcat said. "That is set in stone! And I'm not waiting for it by messenger."

I, THE WORM in Tanili's neck, carry all messages. I read reactions but not thoughts. I can't be sure she has any. I transmit from the top of her spinal column, not from her quadrant or daleth. I'm only the trap door to her 4th brain, but its name isn't fixed. It's the subject of silly argument anyway. Will the term apply to her total capacity or only the top layer? That is a kiwi question. The answer is still green, yet expected before Tanili ripens to full maturity. For now she only radiates and isn't inclined to vocalize, except for halting ambiguous replies, in uncertain imitation of Wildcat, Sierra, and Futura.

Meanwhile I speak for everyone and no one. I must, even if I'm only a trespasser in a transit hub, with energies who have lost their way, to trends I don't understand, with codes I can't interpret. There's no precedence and so much to learn that is not found in a wiki, or an algorithm, to rhythm around, or by way of well-worn grass.

I am blood draws and marrow extracts and sliced from the glands of over-achievers, then catalytically altered, layered onto a carbon-silicon substrate, frozen and cultured in a quantum state. At active body temp I darken, stretch, and curl in shape to be the coil desired. I am a transponder, passing along all signals I receive, in all directions. I am the full path, the synaptic light, not a mere messenger. Across barriers I can amplify the frequency strength that migrates through me. Tanili has no other transmitters. Wave blending, protein sensing, and nerve surges are in my repertoire also. Futura had help from UC San Diego without the other research bio-chemists aware of her deviant purpose. "If I wanted to do this, how would I?" she'd ask. It helped that she'd first married the smartest head in the lab. Divorced now, childless, she couldn't turn to him again.

The gel-like slurry Dr. Futura injected into Tanili was a higher order altered mix from a newly dead baby's brain, basted with nutrients, activators, and accelerants. For years Futura had experimented with mice, fine-tuning the genetic base pairs; growing and re-growing cultures, generation after generation, in bacterial incubators with yeast catalysts for virus delivery. She'd gone from mice to pigs to gibbons, and now to Tanili, nee Vanessa, or vice versa. Dr. Futura had tried radio waves and also low-level radiation, but the results were unpredictable, unrepeatable, and ultimately cremated.

She tried to think in Freudian terms; how would he have defined a fourth level of mind? As a mastery of the first 3 tiers? As a capacitance, for sensory amplification in a future iteration of society? Till this experience was recorded, it was a mistake to speculate, but Dr. Futura hoped to create a new leap and keep it alive. Her goal in playing puppet master was to mutate Tanili into a surprise future, beyond her own comprehension.

Curiously, Futura's father preceded her. He'd been a toy and tool maker with a basement workshop. Every toy he created made the family poorer, as the larger game companies paid him less than his lawyers' fees.

Not able to protect himself, he ended up a suicide, perhaps by accident, when a laser beam burned through his ribs, while testing a cardio-skin used for paint-ball scoring. He'd tried to evolve the material into a 21st century state-of-the-art sheath, as a mock-kill end-game indicator for any sport.

The doctor learned then about an errant gene in her family's bloodline: her eyes were tunnel-focused, without peripheral vision, like her mind. She soon converted her dad's workshop into her own graceland, her princess-opolis, her land of G, to rule the bacteria and yeast offered by mail-order start-ups then, before she found test mice to alter and patent. She tinkered with what her father left behind also. The certified organic return of the plain brown paper bag, that made her so rich, was his un-invention. In fact, his failed successes drove her persistence, her twisted will, and the ironic pinch of her narrow face. To her, tea-totalling other toy ventures would be fine solace if young children outgrew all but her future own living doll.

Decided, the doc acted swiftly, openly. Promising success gained her a coterie among the crowned, seeking new markets.

Immediately she recruited Tanili in a new gourmet diner.

There Tanili, as shrouded as a lost stranger, waited tables. She spent her breaks staring out a window as if waiting for her lover to return. From her sadness it was clear that he wouldn't, and that she might bolt with the first new comer who asked. A $100 tip on a $20 burger jolted loose a wide smile from her flawless, balanced features.

Futura was surprised at how easy it was to ask, "Would you volunteer, if I could change your future? By way of a free ticket to Mars? Or, better yet, if I offered you a 4th brain?"

Tanili removed her waitress apron and sat down quickly, opposite Futura: "Cool! Are you serious? A mind slick? Sick?"

"We'd need to know everything about you, medically."

"Who's we? You're alone."

"My science club. We've no name, but we're of like mind."

"Am I just being slow?" Tanili said, "My body is, I know. It's 2 years behind me in age. I tried biology to find a cure but only learned how to trial out to big pharma for support and that they couldn't, yet I'll live longer, the more delayed I am."

"That's so not abnormal," Futura said. "With us, the risk is enormous and results irreversible, but we can pay. I can help you, regardless. Any questions?"

"I'll trust you, but I will check you out. What's the winning number, my reward?"

"Whatever a new life costs. A million? Ten? You're a lucky find. We're betting you're the jackpot."

"Nice! Just say when then. We're a zillion miles from Earth here, aren't we, last time I looked."

"Where are you from, originally?"

"I blasted-off from a life in Burbank. I'd a future there, I thought, but found out otherwise. It hurts. I'd have been a dancer, but my bones aren't hard enough to take the abuse. Now I've nothing but enthusiasm to offer, and a long neck."

19

"All the better. Tell me about your parents."

"When I was primary school age, they sent me from Eureka down to San Francisco, to live with an uncle and aunt, who took no interest in me. In middle school I couldn't keep up socially, but I was top of class at Lowell High. There's not more to tell, or that I want to tell. I'd far too many embarrassing moments, though no one seemed to notice. So I went south to grow up."

"That's good, as far as it goes, but I want to hear you brag."

"Sorry. I'm not impressed with myself. I'm just passing by. This life and the next will be similar. What do you think? Can I stay here and move at the same time? Will I really live or only be crippled and need your money just to survive?"

"It'll take 9 months to prep you, for the best success rate."

"Will I get pregnant?"

"Definitely not. And don't you make a liar of me. That would be dangerous."

"Having a baby, or crossing you?"

"Both."

"Am I joining a cult?"

"We believe in ourselves, that's true, but I won't make you do anything you don't ordinarily want to."

"I thought I'd have super-powers."

"You might. Or not. It's hard to predict."

"But you said I'd have a 4th brain. Isn't that a screamer?"

"Hadn't occurred to me, that it might not be."

"You do know what you're doing, don't you? Are you just a mad scientist? You have the look."

"Charming!" Futura said, jolted. The project seemed right, till now she'd assumed success. Unplanting an implant might be possible without lasting consequence though. The operation would work, or not, but the sudden creases of fear around Tanili's eyes distressed the doctor deeply.

Yet, in seconds Tanili's face, with it's landscape of twitches and tremors of disbelief and doubt, gave way to long pauses of intrigue and delight. She was ready to grasp the sun now. The rich health of her skin exposed and outshone the dimness of the dining room, as if she gathered light to her.

Still, during the months of preparation, of culturing and reculturing her DNA, no one came looking for her, and she seemed to miss no one. She appeared content with herself, amused to discover, and more fascinated to re-discover, her inner life evolving in wonder, toward an unknowable fate.

Futura and Wildcat puzzled about her: Was she hiding from a husband? Declaring her independence as a runaway? Only 18, she had serious secrets. Jared insisted and Futura agreed, that they needed an ear in her, not so much for the details but to find the mind-bending base-line shaping her.

Thinly sliced from themselves, they created me in advance to monitor conversations between her brains, old and new, An ounce of each of the club of 6, communicating in layered purpose, while listening to Tanili, amplified and interpreted, took months to prepare, but I exist and hear the 6, entangled, talking to each other now, in me in Tanili.

I'm a coiled signal capacitor, and a transfer test of power, yet Tanili's brain doesn't lose power from the transfer. Other forces must hold sway; her brain itself is a Tesla field, though not in his terms, only in effect, or she'd have lightning bolts horning her head, striking down her benefactors. Better than a cave-girl's club perhaps, but not very effective. In essence her 4th brain is self-feeding. Even I, electrified worm that I am, an implant in her long neck, know that. Everyone here does too.

With her mind maturing, the new complexity of her signals means less clarity. I can only delineate the carrier waves, but not what info they bring. When static starts, her mind mutes itself, in a self-limiting way. The noise floor is high enough to suggest radiation is present. Perhaps it's my thorium, even shielded. Definitely, Dr. Futura put limitations into Tanili. She can't run away now or live very long alone, I suspect.

Abruptly it struck me, too often truth is the deliberate reverse of what it seems.

S. Wɪʟᴅᴄᴀᴛ ɪɴᴅᴜʟɢᴇs himself. He's a gusher. Like his refineries, he boasts few scrubbers, but he does buy carbon credits, and his sloganizing has shot him to fame, his first measure of success. His favorite, "Hey Robo, kiss Mars with my rocket fuel, you will never feel a speed bump again," was a big blast 7 years back. Absurdly he has not needed another.

"A slab of a slogan," Sierra said disparagingly.

"A hollow point lie," Jared added.

Not that Wildcat listens. Tanili has given his life new focus. His senses can't escape hers. Obsessing he imagines her leading the way to an unlimited future. Futura knew he'd be trouble. But it was Patagonia who caught him pawing at their patient and exploded, sending him to the hospital for stitches, a tooth sticking out through his cheek. "Next time you stalk or threaten someone, I'll put a bunsen burner up your butt, then send you home to your hapless wife," Patagonia said, still angry.

"You can't expel me. I know too much, and I did nothing."

"Liar!" Pat snapped back. "I've read your signals. Tanili sends them to us."

"Exactly!" Wildcat answered, "She doesn't object to them."

"She doesn't know what they mean yet. We didn't teach her."

Indeed Tanili is a bright unfiltered beacon. We sense each other endlessly in her. It's not good. We need to be able to dial down her signals and turn her off at times, especially since the pulsing is so much stranger now, persistently unrhythmic, an odd resonance from an unknow fundamental. Multiplied by 6 or more. At once, repeatedly. It hurts. Echoes. Eco-echoes. Stop!

"What have we done?" Sierra asked.

"Tanili may be as confused as we are," Patagonia answered.

"Pre-history we had 3 Indias to enjoy at once," India said, "They were the origin of our pleasure in balanced harmonies."

"We're used to a fixed pitch, not your micro-tonal scales."

"Ah, my dear Sierra, both your ears and your mind are out

of tune then, with the natural laws of vibration."

"Not so! You grab a wave, instead of a raft in the riptide?"

"India's being a wistful pixie," Patagonia said. "But Tanili is our group mind. The confusion isn't soothing. She's equipped to handle sensory overload. We're not. She can be of 6 minds at once. The doctor makes mistakes in her presence now. We have to stretch our necks too far, and we can't.

"We need to get her underwater," Futura said

"I won't allow it," Jared answered. "My seed company wants her genes as they are, not tampered with further. Fine-tuned, for certain. Mapped to the entire world and all its variables, sure. But altered to deny her? No!"

"Not used to competition?" Wildcat snapped sharply. "You maybe haven't noticed. Hospitals make their own seed-drugs now and dish them out to patients. The pharmacy cooks up a fixed supply, generics, in small batches. The regs don't cover home scale manufacture. The nurse treating me gave me an inside look. She thought I was a homeless dude, thanks to my cut cheek, my blooded clothes, and dazed state, and rationed out the cheapest biologics."

Jared Planter winced, as if he'd been jabbed in the ribs.

"Not a joke!" Wildcat said. "Count the links they've snipped away from your subsidiaries."

"I vote that we take our chances," Sierra said.

"I agree," Wildcat offered.

Jared nodded reluctantly. Futura too. India asked for a short delay to gather outside information. Not a chance. This underground lab is its own research center.

The decision to advance regardless carried by majority, but we still need to wait, to test again, to get more acquainted with each other, to climb, even fearfully, to the next bright ledge, with Tanili.

She's a diamond, only dimmed by our concerns. We're still in love with her sparkle, however flawed her future might be. Yet, everything is in doubt.

WITHOUT KNOWING WHY, Tanilli sought a rabbit hole. To find its opening, she waited till the middle of the night, then explored. A pressure-sprung door opened to a second, smaller, operating theater, dusty, seemingly abandoned.

From the shadows a tall gaunt man with a deep frown and a swollen head, in a blue hospital gown and pushing an IV stand with a tube to his arm, stepped to her. His shuffle showed no threat. She had surprised him more, it seemed.

"Dr. Pippen, I presume, I presume," he said anxiously. "Are we married? Were we? I'm Severly. I was. I am. I don't know. I'm Ilya Severly. I'm Ill Scientist. No. I don't know. I have aphasia, or its cousin, futuria, I don't know, I'm told, I will never get better. I try. My wife has my name. Sometimes."

'Futura failed you. You should have a new brain. Instead the old is damaged.'

Her mind realigned around the thought. She had a head start. She needed to escape.

"Do you live here?" She asked.

"I do, I don't know. I have a door."

After a 10 minute search, feeling the smooth walls for vibrations, she found it. On the other side a wide-shouldered attendant stretched out asleep in a chair next to a hospital bed. On the bedside table in easy reach lay a thick black belt with mace, a long flashlight, and a radio, but no gun.

Ready to challenge him, she reached for the belt. Slow footsteps echoed behind her. She froze, then ran back to the main room. Severly didn't follow her. She closed his door tightly.

In the morning, Dr Futura sensed a change in Tanili, an undefined fear that shook the doctor's confidence.

TANILI IS a tattoo on the gloom now. Her needles define no pattern. Her promise isn't painful; her 4th brain is alive, inking itself in disguise. At each step closer to her, we feel more distant. She's transmogrifying, inwardly. As her voice node, I say so.

Futura uses blood draws to adjust the meds, but she wants to put a translator into me in turn. "Our odd bean chats at us in signals we can't interpret. It's unnerving."

"Yank the vanilla bug out," Patagonia said. "Or easier, just don't listen. Below deck in a ship at sea, you get used to the fog horns and the rolling."

"But weather is measureable," Sierra answered. "We can read Tanili's bio-inks too. Her oscilloscope readings speak. But not 2 things correlate. Day to day she's 10 ways different."

Gradually though, staring endlessly at the monitors, we began seeing the veiled repeats, and ourselves in them. Sierra is sure she's jagged; India is a long wave; Patagonia is a lashing line; and Futura a fuzzy blur; but Wildcat is a drumbeat, and Jared a thinning constellation. Tanili is a spectral offset, that's certain. Mostly we see our frustration.

Yet, Tanili's grace is visible: she floats, as if on stage, hanging in the heavy air. Her new brain lifts her now. She seems to rise forever before drifting back to earth. She keeps to no routine.

At times she struggles, more like a nail rising out of a plank floor, but her shining and the depth of her darkening eyes surprise us still. Her silence is unnerving. She won't speak to us.

This isn't what we expected. It goes against the grain of a 4th brain. Strangely she appears to be communicating but not with us, or with her voice, nor in any recognizable language.

We've bombarded her with algorithms and arguments, the tools of logic, but they've no apparent effect. Stalled, without evident certainty, our group is drifting apart. Only this wily bean is holding us together. We talk to each other through him, even when we don't want to. We've no choice.

In our growing silence, together we're losing sight of ourselves as well. Wildcat's windsor-knotted short wide ties, India's paisley saris, and Futura's off-white waist coats, as she bustles in and out of her clean side-rooms with their antiseptic UV lights, go unnoticed now.

Sierra in forest camouflage is also adrift. She constantly talks to Siri, Apple's concierge for queries, but gets no help, yet Siri's masters may suspect what's happening here, as Sierra hides nothing in her quest for robotic answers.

Jared in his sweat suits jauntily runs the quiet treadmill belts, as if he were in space and hoping to preserve his bones.

Bravely Wildcat still taunts Patagonia, with inspired slogans about next-gen petro-chem and self-healing science. He thrives on her challenges. "Tanili's an oh-so-fine example of WeChem!" he said.

"Don't push it!" Patagonia snapped. "You'll lose the rest of your teeth."

Wildcat is irrepressible. He clearly lusts after Tanili. He's still selling himself, to claim her. Patagonia's assault oddly elevated him. The gash in his cheek promises an intriguing scar.

Daily now, our group of 6 takes breaks outside beyond the barn, burning rotting firewood, filled with segmented white maggots, good for cleaning wounds and creating kindling. The burning fascinates Tanili. She joins us silently. I, the bean, hear her airy thoughts in fragments now, but don't pass them on.

She wonders why her awareness is limited to here, and why it can't be everywhere, or at least somewhere else, far beyond her eyes' reach. Her new brain is shaped like a dome, or urn upside down, filling up the space between her old brain and her skull, yet she senses life at the horizon, and as distant as our moon. She should be able to live in 6 time-frames at once. She's receiving new signals herself, not through me, and doesn't know from where. Nor do I. There's no guessing.

Her food seems to be part of the formulary. She picks and chooses and improves. After all, she did control the diner menu, but the doubts don't disappear. "Will she live? Jared asked.

"Did we fail?" Sierra asked.

"How can you ask? My purpose is pure," Futura said.

"What exactly does that mean?" Wildcat asked.

"I did an autopsy on my sister and harvested her organs," Futura said. "She hung herself. Her husband didn't believe it was suicide. I agreed and set out to prove he killed her. I failed, only because the evidence was ambiguous. Here I only have one goal, the best tools, and a single mind-set. Tanili will live, because I've decided she will. Faith has its rewards."

The revelation shocked the group. They went silent.

"Tact in Impact!" Tanili suddenly said, surprising everyone.

"Wow! Is she worth it!" Wildcat answered with a smile wider than his tie. "She listens to me after all, I knew it!"

Sierra and Patagonia, startled, nearly choked in panic.

"Talk to me! I created you," Futura demanded of Tanili.

"She'll be my new top banner!" Wildcat said.

"You're not putting her on your signs," Jared said, appalled. "It'd be obscene —"

"What'd you think? We knew exactly what we'd be getting into," India interrupted. "Tanili will have to learn, as we've done, to protect our planet. We've work to do. I'll teach her to be our Earth Mother, first."

Wildcat laughed: "Yeah, that's two heads, six arms and sucker legs. A flailing octopus to you, but a gold god-rod to me!"

Sierra whacked him on his left ear with her open palm.

He fled, smiling, his pleasure in the perverse still intact.

Jared paced, wincing repeatedly, still appalled, wondering how to take charge, but unable to find his way.

Though the foremost seed giant, thanks to green science, he preferred camping alone, pruning, chopping mature wood, and stoking a fire. To him the grain of polished burl is infinitely variable. Tall and thin, like an over-watered sprout, Jared often tested himself against the random chaos of distant jungles, where strange lives prevail, each in its own niche, where straight lines don't survive, as often as they're attempted.

Here, the women in this group appeal to him at times, but there isn't a natural among them. An expert's knife has recarved them all, but they're afraid to alter their genetic layerings. They once hoped to share Tanili's brain, but life has slid toward chaos, spiced with abuse. Common sense seems to've been abandoned. Logic too. as well as blood and electro-magnetic measurements. We've nothing to guide us. The future is ever more unknown, but not frightening, yet.

In creating Tanili, we focused on higher awareness beyond boundaries and spectral sensitivities, not on taking aggression to the next level, even for self-preservation. We didn't add shielding or encase or alter her to protect ourselves either. Not that we could have easily, or be certain of a set outcome. What is ahead now is perhaps more chance than choice. But that was the point: if we knew what was likely, we wouldn't have done it. The risks of adventure excited us to action, more than the rewards, though none of us admitted that. We openly believe though, that the risks entitle us to the full rewards.

Enough said. Although, come to think of it, the doctor's Satellite Mice, as she nicknamed them, to suggest success in higher orbit, did work in their own right. Tanili herself is our only guide to knowing now. It hasn't occurred to anyone yet, that through me she feels the 6 of us to be part of herself. Communication is a 2-way street. Patagonia has her sub-strates, invisible physics makes sure of that.

For Doc Futura, though, a pressing question weighs heavily: Will Tanili's brain, once fully formed, self-renew and regenerate indefinitely.

Of course, nothing is permanent — we know that too.

The 6 in this club don't hear Tanili, really.

I do, or think I do, and don't tell anyone. I've a choice. I've given myself one. Though in theory I'm only an amalgam, in mind and body, I manage nicely.

Strange to be so one, and independent. For everyone.

TANILI WAS WORRIED. Little had shape to her, only sensation.

Her reasoning was erratic. Severly was only the shadow now. Her memory denied him.

She didn't understand her confusion, even when her mind was most clear. She came out of her coma not thinking at all, to an unclouded awareness. Gradually the forms around her defined themselves, the 6 people too. Soon she became aware of her thinking, that she could guide it, act on it, and smile with it. Within weeks, she could think without thinking: yet, every thought came with a feeling, a resonance that seemed right. She drifted effortlessly wanting to float forever, beyond imagining.

She often listened to the 6 without hearing them.

"We have to teach her to say 'no' and 'not me'," Sierra said.

"We're winning! We're so winning!" Tanili sang suddenly, hopping up and down, swinging her arms side to side in a high school cheerleader chant, that popped to the surface abruptly.

Dismayed, Futura felt betrayed by Tanili's throw-back act. Futura and Patagonia had just discussed how to separate out the micro-crystals found in an amorphous material, that disrupt its solubility, to achieve the purest brain. The adjacent lab with its atomic force microscope, distillation oven and all else needed to bypass patent filings and licensing fees, allowed the 6 to enter this research garden, to build on existing blocks, to play in the greenhouse of life, They realized now that their problems were not only in the chemistry, but in the other fixed substrate, the lives Tanili had led before, which they knew little about and so could not predict from.

At the same time a rush of memories surrounded Tanili. Deeply distressed she kneeled, hammered to the ground in horror by them. She'd been married quite young to a plastic surgeon, who'd transformed her but also threatened to take back her looks when she left him. He could still be hunting her. Her mind leaped to escape, but she found herself watching down, as if from the balcony in the basement operating theater. Though evolved and enhanced in undefined ways she felt unchanged by the doctor's treatment. Her fears intensified. Were these women surrounding her part of her husband's plot to take away her mind as well as her face?

They could reclaim her brain without her husband's help. She knew, she felt that fragile, denied the doctor's promised gift of super-powers. That belonged to other women, it seemed.

Tanili curled inwardly, bristling, longing for help.

A year earlier, her detour into dance brought admirers, Cran especially, who she'd depended on, but he'd dropped out of sight. A shy, sharp youth with inventive talent, he was the photographer who'd developed her. Cran, short for Cranberry or Cranium, depending on which parent you asked, had a secure future of his choosing, waiting in San Francisco. His large head would have magnetized a movie audience but he preferred to be behind the camera, deciding how the world should see, whether in gold or silver chloride, or digitally. He felt no need to be in the picture if the scene was his. Tanili had crafted herself for him, with her fluid grace, her naivete. She adopted her vaguely Scottish accent from her uncle. But Cran didn't intend to detour after her, or deny himself.

His father, a museum photographer and platinum master, was the last living link to the art's immortals. Cran nonetheless surpassed his father in technique and applied for a patent to print in gold by way of molecular manipulation. Encapsulating gold salts at different sizes leads to different colors and potentially to an image-coated space craft that might last till dark matter scraped it off.

Tanili guessed that Cran and his dad were in Washington now, but they could just as easily be flying over Nebraska, without her knowing, trying to figure out the best way to communicate with aliens. Lasting space travel was their focus. She knew that an ex-White House photographer had invited them to DC. Adam Q by name, or an alias similar, headed a provoking mental group called White Men of America, that wasn't completely white, but held its own council: they didn't want to rule anyone or be ruled in turn; they simply wanted the wonder of the universe to be theirs, without Earth, if necessary, and without the renegade Russians, who had their own agenda, spraying poisons and seeding discontent to settle old scores, rather than tap the natural resources of Siberia, as it thawed freely.

For a brief moment, Tanili felt her fears to be groundless. Everything fit together in her favor. She could weave a web around herself, see through clouds, yet find firm footing, while not having to know anything. She was sure, the glass monitors along the periphery of the room offered a possibility of escape. The internet gives everyone an identity within an identity within an identity, yet it can't flower up life in even the richest farm dirt. Still, the screens suggested a root idea, as she could scan and retain them all at once. She sensed the people in the room similarly, with their collective stare and realized suddenly, she had her own power over the 6, not because she understood, but because they didn't, though they identified with her; even the men did. Their eyes followed hers. They twitched at her every movement. The 6 were peas locked in their skull pods, but her mind was free to wander as far as it wished, if she had the will to escape, to reach past the pale grasping walls. Yet, she remained standing among the 6, because one, the doctor, kept a distance and projected her own sense of control, however uncertain.

Futura and Patagonia remained analytical. Frowning at each other, they argued about printing with live stem cells on alternate substrate. "The secret is in adding egg yolk and sugar to the mix, as accelerators, and not using platinum or gold as catalysts," Futura said.

'Could they hear her thoughts without realizing it?' Tanili wondered. 'These people are all so deep in their rabbit holes that they've lost sight of their sun. Yet, the gangly man among

31

them is more sprout than root, more likely to blossom outright.'

She sensed his ills, a sewn hernia, a glass eye, a trimmed prostrate, but he carried himself proudly, being the 5th great grandson of a revolutionary president, and he was rich beyond measure, as he owned a key source of life. Jared told none of this to her, but it set his thinking and was never out of mind. Tanili talked to him in her thoughts, asking for help, but he didn't hear her.

The second man was a knot of intrigue, climbing his own rope, whipping himself upward, with a long reach, all skin and bones like a hungry frog, given to croaking, as his throat kept tensing. "In my world, good slogans tell us the Why behind the What-the-Fuck!" he announced.

"You want to translate that?" Sierra asked.

"Only if I've a free hand, when we make Tanili public."

"Not happening, you know that."

"Not likely to either," India said. "What's not right?"

"And when will we know?" Sierra said. "The weather's near normal this year, and the season's on time. That's encouraging at least. It'd help us, Doc, to know the exact DNA map that you're keeping so secret."

"Simple. My base camp was third brain enhanced. I tried undifferentiated stem cells, ganglions, eels, and other electrically active origins, but none worked as well as the normal, modified in a petri dish under the microscope, with new genetic letters of course."

"What do your mice tell you here?" Jared asked.

"Nothing. Mice don't menstruate. They can't tell us anything about a real live woman."

The 6 analyzed the doc's thinking, as if all had gone wrong.

Whether Tanili was a flub, a muddle or a deadly disaster wasn't clear yet. If she needed more time, they could give that to her. Definitely though, if her brains didn't integrate, if they couldn't talk to each other, she'd end up a 2-headed monster fighting for control of her only body.

"My idea is to have a brain grow its own body, if we reach the next level beyond this," Patagonia said. "There, thoughts are broken symmetries, competing, toward a new harmonic convergence."

"I've played with that concept in theory," the doc said, "but first we need to master mRNA, our code for universal temporary instruction. Through it, we can convert DNA into permanent dynamic proteins."

"Isn't that a contradiction?" India asked.

"That's our strength, being contrary," Wildcat said smartly.

"He's right. We're on the road to wisdom," Patagonia said.

'You've arrived, but don't know it,' Tanili wanted to answer, but didn't, as she couldn't explain why. Maybe it wasn't true.

"Don't men and women have different brains?" India asked.

"Yeah, when you criticize girls, they cry," Wildcat said.

"Wildcat's not the idiot he seems," Patagonia affirmed. "The opposite assumption, of identical brains, is also ideology, however."

"Did you take that into account, Doc?" Sierra asked.

Tanili waited for a reply, but there was none.

CRAN SHARPENED in Tanili's memory. His round face with its dimpled chin smiled at her longingly. To her, excitedly he repeated his plans. "The orbiting cities on my drawing board show overlords prowling the sky, searching to commercialize low orbit space. Nasa's spear-like planes, with fins for wings, without sonic booms are my prototype. I need minds now like yours in the sky, able to read every instrument at once, to decide instantly, to create and police our new world. Later you can rule it indifferently, leaving each to his own success, or yours, if you wish." Had he said this to her before? He must have, but couldn't have.

She tried to answer him, by way of entanglement, radio frequencies, inner whispers, and packets of code. She'd learned a lot, without realizing it, in her 6 months with the cluster of 6 around her. But Cran didn't respond newly. He only repeated himself. She heard him as a drum beat, a syncopated signal that dizzied her now.

The next voice was the doctor's: "I need suction! Her brain's bleeding! Quick! It's swelling up."

Strapped down, Tanili struggled to free herself. The doctor was taking Cran from her, with her brain and face. She was sure he'd be crippled and die with her. She screamed. The shock numbed her. She went deaf. The bleeding slowed. Still, the operating table did not release her.

The 6 backed away in horror at Tanili's contortions and her bloodied hair. Jared stopped the doctor. "She's okay!" he said, pleading desperately. "She's just trying too hard. She doesn't know how to use her new brain. Confusion is crazing her. Let her be! The bleeding's stopping."

The doctor pushed him aside, furious. "She's my patient! I decide. That's right. I decide!" Patagonia restrained Dr. Futura, both hands on her neck. "Do you want to be sewn up like Wildcat? No, I didn't think so. Back off!"

In the morning, before dawn, Tanili broke her bonds and escaped, feeling her way to freedom. The oozing in her scalp had stopped. The diner where she'd waitressed gave her a chance to clean up. With permission she hid in the owner's apartment. Unsettled but comfortable, curious but decidedly cautious, she kept watch at the window for any pursuers.

She discovered them in the *Wall Street Journal*. Captions under photos of the 6 declared them missing and hinted at a possible conspiracy in the works; after all the 6 disappeared at the same time regularly, which suggested a plan to surprise the public with one new scheme or another. Definitely they had to be together, perhaps at a very private island somewhere. They owned enough of them.

Cran, his dad, provocateur Adam-Q, his wife Nori, and her stunning sister Celestina also appeared, identified, in a single photo of the latest up-to-being-seen in Washington. Searing pangs of jealousy at the sight of Cran and Celestina, eyeing each other in a trendy restaurant, overwhelmed Tanili. She wanted to break the pair back to its parts somehow. It might be easy, now that she had so much more to offer. Did she? Really, she felt like Kobe beef, tenderized alive, before being killed, cooked and served to connoisseurs: it was the top special on the diner's catering menu. Japanese tariff-avoiding companies had put down roots nearby. Visiting executives enjoyed the home taste.

But Tanili was not offering herself to anyone again, for any purpose but protection. Was perfection possible, she wondered.

REPORTERS LIKE to make people sound as if they're spilling dirt on themselves. That's the essence of the press. Lindell had 20 years experience at it, but Lin, as she was called locally, had much too many items hanging on her ears at the moment: glasses, earrings, hearing aids, and a smog mask. The nearby drug factory was having a bad day, and Lin was distracted. Nonetheless, she recognized Wildcat as soon as he entered the diner door. He was always good for a quote, even if his profanity wasn't printable.

But why was he in town? Lin wondered. Rumor had it, he lived in the Caribbean, maintaining his tan, not here nursing new scars on his face. A roughneck he started out and still was.

"How're they hanging?" Lin asked, and motioned him to sit in the booth with her. "You're holding out on me. I met you in Dallas at a drilling convention. Remember? We'd a good time."

"It'd help if you took off your mask," he snapped.

"Take yours off too, and we can talk."

"You're that reporter! You quoted me when I was shit-faced."

"But you got the head-line. Ink is good. No such thing as bad publicity, remember?"

He plumped himself down and stared intently at her.

"So what's fate have in store for you today?" Lin asked.

"My Karma is not a camel-faced cunt," Wildcat said bluntly.

Lin smashed a bowl of onion soup against his forehead. He slumped in the seat. Lin retreated out the door. Tanili, watching from the kitchen, ready to run to Wildcat, stopped herself.

A public revealing might be dangerous. She stepped back. Pilot waves, decoherence, and many-worlds, all ideas from Patagonia's physics, took hold of Tanili's mind but didn't give her new perspective. She wasn't ready for a 5th brain. Her 4th was enough trouble, clearly. The resonance of Wildcat's assault was enlightening though. At the mercy of this still-existing culture, she needed to destroy it before it damaged her further.

It had reason to deny her, as an alien among the ordinary.

She tried to define herself, to judge her weapons. Her new brain had begun as plasma, but it'd gelled, for sure, into orbits of possibility. Assets were clarity in complexity, greater speed of awareness, and the fine resonance she felt, but if there were no delays or pauses in her mind now, it also stumbled into error more quickly. Her freely spinning energy hadn't found critical mass. The lights in her brain had switched on but didn't know what they were seeing or how they might scale. Super-computer status wasn't hers. If she was now a quantum well instead, she had yet to taste the luminescent waters.

"Of course, interacting lattice vibrations might explain a few things." Patagonia said so.

Yes, Patagonia spoke. Tanili startled. The bug, it had to be the bug. The 6 were implanted at the base of her brain. She linked to them, whether she liked it or not, and she couldn't cut them out without killing herself. She didn't have the skill.

The police and an ambulance arrived for Wildcat. No one admitted to being a witness. Tanili hid in the garage apartment of the diner's owner. Well-known, his head shaved, so that he didn't have to wear a hair net in the kitchen, he ran her errands for her now, for a small fee, which translated into 20K when he brought the rest of her 2 million dollar reward to her, in cash from her safety deposit box at the bank. As patient and guinea pig she had earned it. She sewed the thousand dollar bills into the lining of 2 suitcases, bought a bus ticket to Washington, dyed her hair 2 shades toward brown and promptly left town.

Feeling vulnerable, she obsessed with her luggage and her inability to exercise the powers the cash promised. It could not go through airport security.

THEN AGAIN, her brain had just been born, when her Neander-thals came knocking. In retreat, she knew without thinking, primitives held 1000 fears that they needed to appease. Ritual allayed most of them. Tanili too inherited her alarm with the rest of her spine and had to will her way forward now without help, without a ghost ancestor to guide her.

Her true shaman was in DC. Of that, she was certain.

The bus ride was rougher than she expected, much slower than the speed of thought too. She called ahead to Cran. Celestina answered his cell, identifying herself. Tanili hung up, not ready to compete.

The trip was long, but Union Station offered a fine example of city cave-life. The hard wooden bench in the waiting hall gave her time to obsess more. Her asymmetry distressed her. Her brain was in a constantly excited state, thinking fractionally. She'd heard the doctor talking about altering her base pairs into spin triplets. Tanili could only guess what that meant. She was still sure, that Futura operated intuitively and experimentally, while Patagonia labored with theories to a private purpose, hunched around her thoughts, but willing to lash out like a whip at any insult or obstacle. Patagonia was her own 5th brain in the making, tightly disciplined, unpredictable, frightening.

Tanili 2-fingered her wrist to take her pulse. 70. Normal.

Her anxieties were still undefined, a constant state of mind.

She scanned the waiting room chaos, then focused intently on two travelers with backpacks across the aisle: a couple, content with each other, indifferent to everyone else. Suddenly they weren't. They jumped up, agitated, and left in opposite directions. Was this Tanili's doing? How could it be?

She called Cran again, got his DC address now, and set off to visit him in his camp at a garden house belonging to Adam-Q, an ex-White House camera-man and sly provocateur on the Beltway scene. *The Washington Postal* railed against him. His pamphlets created dedicated enemies. After he called a senior senator "a hair-ball in the bureaucratic sewer," the death-threats started. He also was the voice of a space-native club, Aliens of America; there he only whispered. Really, this futurist club was a podium without a platform. It existed solely to guarantee an audience for Adam's arrows, wherever they struck. His fans wanted to pick his targets, but he could paint a bull's eye on anyone, and, in doing so, often inspired his victims to heal and improve and be true challenges. So said *The Postal*.

In fact Adam-Q's wonder in life was his wife Nori. Trained by Nasa, she failed to make astronaut, yet all who came to her house shared the same lust for the extra-terrestial. Cran's platform tent in the backyard had a mesh top that let the stars in.

He hugged Tanili tightly to him, genuinely glad to see her. Her radiance overwhelmed him. In Cran's arms, she wanted to collapse forever, but his crisp smile, confidence, and elan revived her. She wasn't sure what to tell him, whether he could see her changes. "I've come for your help and to give you mine. What do you most want, besides me?" she asked coyly.

"To have a constant named after me, like the speed of light, or Avogadro's number, at the least." He was serious. "I'd settle for a distant galaxy," he added.

"Wouldn't you rather re-invent the universe?" Tanili asked.

"That's too ambitious," he said.

"Or be the square root of time, the next generation of life?"

Cran's eyes went wide. "You've changed. You never thought like this. You didn't understand me at all before."

"I didn't know that I did," Tanili said happily.

They stood quietly with the tall trees and sheltering shrubs.

"What's Avogadro's number?" Celestina interrupted.

"This is Nori's little sister," Cran said, "Meet Tanili."

"I've known Cran since I was born," Tanili said.

"Simply put," Cran said, eying both women for approval, "A's number is a law: the number of molecules of all gases will be the same in a given space. That doesn't seem right but it is."

"Are we as plain and simple for you?" Tanili offered.

"Speak for yourself," Celestina said.

"I am. And I'm willing to challenge you when you're ready."

"I don't need to compete."

"We all do," Tanili said, "but I've an advantage."

"You knew Cran before me?"

"That too. I met him at my birth, every one of them."

"Well, he thinks you'll make a good manikin for my lotions and potions. That's what I do, create them, big league."

"Do they heal? Or are they just fashionable?" Tanili asked.

"If you need healing, I can help," Celestina said, intent on seizing the advantage.

Tanili smiled indulgently. She waited, as if Celestina had missed her cue and required a prompter and stage directions.

"I've been developing *Tears of Wine* for a lover to lick off the wearer's cheek," Celestina offered, "Cran loves the taste on me. But it's different for men who don't have the nose."

"Excuse me," Cran said, blushing, and hurried to the house.

"You've been worked on," Celestina said to Tanili, shocking her. "It was an expensive job, I can tell, but why did you need it so young?"

Tanili freaked. She wasn't ready to reveal herself to this stranger.

"You okay? I didn't mean to insult you. Not really," Celestina said. Relentlessly charming, she held an edge.

Cran returned with 3 tall glasses of lemon soda water, "To quench the randomness," he said.

Celestina sniffed at the drink. "The odor released, as the bubbles pop, influences the perception of flavor. I could trick and treat people with this all day."

Adam-Q joined them. "You may already know, astronauts on the space station once studied the bubbles in soda, hoping to stop the bloating they cause. The bubbles join but don't rise inside. It can get gastrically nasty."

"But right now I'm the dinner bell," he added blandly.

"ADAM-Q HAS his own quantum signature," Patagonia said. "But he's really a giggler." Tanili heard her. She was certain. Or was it the vanilla-bean in her neck mouthing Patagonia again?

For certain, the bean bug was developing its own memory and personality. It still carried every threat the 6 made. Tanili couldn't deny, let alone quiet, them.

She needed a new doctor, not one self-righteously wrong like India, who had never finished her studies anyway. Adam-Q's astronaut-trained wife, Nori, offered her expertise. No, no, it was India talking, disguising herself by way of the bean.

Tanili circled the house, turning every 6 steps to confront her ghosts, calling on her new brain to defeat them. The green brick arches in the log and glass 2-story structure distracted her. A master architect had planned every detail. Tanili tried a like-thinking blueprint, walling in each voice in its own room. The 6 went silent, clawing at their plate glass prisons.

No get-out-of-jail-free passes existed, and none would, if Tanili won the contest the 6 had created.

Clearly, Cran, involved with Celestina now, was no longer available to help. However recently it happened, Cran had no choice, or wasn't allowing himself one, yet he was tempted, it seemed. Tanili fretted, unsure what to tell him and uncertain of what he might do. What aid did she need, she wondered, and why? She didn't actually have to hide. The 6 did, in truth.

Though she was given a guest room in the house, she buried one suitcase under the floor of the platform tent as backup and went exploring. She needed her own island. Yet, she already was floating in every direction at once, beyond the horizon, back to herself, freely. She could levitate in her mind also, or shrink to a worm in the leaf mold. She heard a garden snake slithering, then digesting a mouse, or thought she did. A beautiful red fox trotted past, with just a glance at her. She tried to stop him with her thoughts. She couldn't.

Back in the house, at dinner, over goat cheese Greek salad, Tanili posed as a hypothetical problem for Cran.

"If outer space were a 4th brain that each of us carried inside, what would life be like?" she asked.

He dropped his fork. "That will happen someday," he said.

"Suppose it already has, to different degrees in other people, how would we live?" Tanili persisted.

"It's true for me already," Nori said suddenly. "I feel defeated and denied because I was dropped from the program after 2 years of training."

"Suppose you weren't dropped but never sent on a rocket, yet your mind could take you anywhere and integrate your being there with your daily life here, then what?"

"I'd probably go mad," Nori said.

"Not if you had a 4th brain to help you," Tanili said.

"I can't imagine it. Our government grants don't advocate an evolutionary approach. The brain is one integrated organ with its own integrity. We don't like to fund growing proteins that don't exist in nature. We aid very few universities making macro-molecules of our neuro-identity. Brains don't aggregate easily, so research depends on slicing the results thinner and thinner to keep them oxygenated and alive, even on a glass slide. Maybe elsewhere it's different."

"Do you know what the Chinese are doing?" Celestina asked.

"We have our suspicions," Nori said.

"Put 2 sisters together. They're of one mind," Adam-Q said.

Cran decided then and there, to solve the mystery of Tanili. She had the reach he liked to seek. What kind of constant might emerge? Maybe it wouldn't speak for the universe. Did it much matter? She could hear him thinking, but she shifted to Adam: "You've done executive portraits. Are my patrons among them?"

She named the 6. Adam shook his tall head and scrunched up his face. "Does poetry inspire your patrons? Not even Haiku poo? They can always look for themselves in the mirror to find a frolic or 2, but here, listen up. I've something else for you."

Relaxing, winging it, in a feathery voice, with barely a pause, he went on, "Wander through windows, let your mind grow, turn down the podcast, get lost in the snow, yet see the grass growing, the seeds blowing, lofting in spirals of hope. Walk to the beach, find a killer whale on our continental slope. An ocean of biting belief is tastier than a best mope. Love what your ears tell you. Atone for your excess and haste. Love with your eyes and flush your neurotoxic waste with peach soap. Recycle your blood into the finest 2-photon trope...."

Adam stopped, crashing, choking on his own laughter.

She expected him to say more. "That's a gastriloquy," he said finally, "Lettuce head poetry, with potential, but with 4 brains, instead of a 4-course salad in me, I could do better. Now tell us your story."

The bean in her neck screamed: 'They're killing me. They're killing me. Trying to. You too. Let me live. I want to live!'

Tanili clasped her thin hands to her ears and slapped at her face and abruptly sat still, as if nothing had happened.

"There a problem?" Cran said calmy, as if all were normal, "You see, we assume, brains are self-cleaning. Oxidized output removes itself in sleep, we think, but we don't know what we can't see. Complexity isn't always singular. How can we stay pure and simple, and deal with every last detail?"

"Let nature take its course," Celestina said, her green eyes sparkling. "Enhanced, of course, if there's a chance, is my big preference."

"Everything has its place in the brain atlas," Adam said.

"Definitions are still our un-doing," Cran said, "Will you change the words, if I can alter the reality?"

"I don't have the skill. Tanili is a cool investigative start though. Advances often begin with accidents," Adam said.

"I like kiss-cutting myself," Celestina went on.

"Are we talking castration?" Nori asked.

"Only my sister'd think that," Celestina said.

"And who you compete with defines you," Nori said. "Desert

anyone? I apologize, not for the puddings, but the tarts. Too sweet. I put in sugar to feed the yeast."

"Sister, sister, don't apologize. The poorer bees always steal their honey from the best hives. You owe me, sister, for making Cran's ex-mistress a guest here."

Tanili smiled to herself. She and Cran were never lovers, but the possibility now was real. Her hands shook. Her orange drink spilled. She had no control over herself. The dangers inside her multiplied. Treading the edge of a fragile ledge was nerve-wracking. She needed to hide far away till her mind stopped fracturing. "Deciding what to pack for a trip to Mars is a better start," she said.

"I sleep on my left side with blackout shades to drain my brain of the ß-amyloids that build up in daylight," Nori said. "Nasa doesn't teach that yet."

"They eject their dirty laundry in flames from the space station too," Adam-Q said.

"I should be volunteering for life on a different planet," Tanili said.

"Would you like to join the program? I can get you a head-start. A physical is the first step, after a mental test, after a long questionnaire," Nori said.

"I'd need to demagnetize my brain first," Tanili said. "Quiet the force fields."

"Allow me," Cran said, and took her outside for a back rub.

"Why does Adam call his club *White Men of America*, when anyone can join?" Tanili asked.

"It was the quickest way to get banned," Cran answered.

CRAN HUNCHED over Tanili as she sat on the floor of his platform tent. Quickly he discovered the scars on her neck and the uneven skin. "You've strange lumps here. From an accident?"

"A tracking implant," she admitted, "Can you help me get rid of it?"

"Wow! You're serious. Well, we can modify it to give a false signal and see who comes looking. No? You mean you hear it?"

"I may be able to send my own messages," she answered, deciding to trust Cran to a point. "Perhaps take control even, but I'm in trouble. The intentions of my patrons are uncertain, in conflict, and independent of me. The implant is theirs."

Cran stared at her skeptically. "Your benefactors are superstars in their fields. If they want a handle on you, they have it. How did you find them?"

"They picked me, opportunistically, and paid well. I agreed to their experiment."

"To monitor the effect of the ungodly wet heat they cause? To send you to Mars? Humans on Mars will bring our worst problems with them. We won't escape ourselves. Or will we? You have changed, but I, well, you're vulnerable, and inviting, and I —"

"I'm not ready for you," Tanili said. "My mind has to heal. My brain is new to me. I've past lives but they're not mine anymore. Don't ask me to explain. You're not ready for me either."

"I'm up for anything, just let me know. Should we get the implant out? It's better done in a hospital, or don't you want the law involved?".

"Not now, or ever," Tanili answered.

"I know eco-terrorists, mid-ladder on the money scale. They own scary companies, but they're secret do-gooders. They've the resources if we need them, to combat your patrons, or at least force them publicly to take sides. What say?"

"I just want to remake my own world."

"Wrong answer. Everything matters. Earth is irreplaceable."
"So am I."

"I agree. Let's get you fixed then," Cran said, and called Redbud and Glory, retired eco-bombers who helped good shadow causes still, though they owned a thriving lumber company. Their plan to blow up the Chinese tree-free paper trade, to slow its silicon plastic ash was in progress. "Hazardous waste has a place on Pluto" was their slogan.

Redbud and Glory in turn called around and found a general surgeon in DC who agreed to help, in his private office, but he sewed up his incisions when he saw the attaching weave, afraid he'd paralyze Tanili. Cran urged him to treat the implant as a tumor and disable it at the least. The surgeon refused. "Her scans aren't clear. There's more going on here than I understand. I've no history to work from. Her spine's fully involved. I can't take the chance. Go back to the people who did this."

Out from anesthesia, Tanili squabbled with the surgeon irritably. "There are advanced techniques here I'm unfamiliar with," the surgeon insisted. "Go to the congressional hospital. They've seen it all." Tanili was tempted to part her hair and show him the wax-filled hole in her skull above her ear.

Cran grew more curious. "Someone experimented on you at great expense, expertly. He won't let you go easily. Tell me."

"Not till I'm free of this implant monitoring me —"

"I suspect it has a life of its own now," Cran said. "If I'm right, you're a trans-human treasure. Yes?"

"More than you know. Less than you think. One op at a time, please."

Back at Adam and Nori's home, in the greenhouse, Cran and Tanili found Celestina in white cowboy boots, trimming oversized marijuana buds. "These are a sideline. They've their own cachet and keep their own council. My company is very selective about its controversies.," she explained. "They don't mind face cream made of stem cells from infant foreskins collected during mass circumcisions, though. I can get you both a free sample."

"You can say no, you won't help, but we need a good surgeon who has a private clinic off the grid," Cran said.

"For you, anything," Celestina said, with a wink and a sneer. "But she hasn't lent her tit to our gallon of milk. She owes. Get my drift?"

"Expectation is everything," Tanili said. "Your lotions and potions will be in my thoughts, forever spoiled."

"I'll see what I can do then," Celestina said seriously.

Within 24 hours, TT showed up. A short wiry man in ceaseless motion, he chopped out his words quickly as if desperate for the burn of their heat. He found Tanili alone in Cran's tent. "Name's Talent. I've a knack for all things man-made. I got 3 calls to assist you. Cran around?"

"He's working with Adam-Q on new mission statements for space colonies," Tanili said. "Do you know what I need?"

"No, but I know what my clients want. You'll come with me quietly. Let's go!"

"No way. Who gave you orders?"

"The government. Not ours, but you never know. The likely is possible too. It's my job to potentiate the paid reality."

"What's that mean? Specifics, please, or I'm going nowhere."

He grabbed her left arm and swung her into a chokehold. Within a minute, she was bound, gagged, blind-folded, and slung over his shoulder on the way to his van in broad daylight. No one intervened. The leafy street was empty.

"You're in demand," TT said in the van. "I should auction you to the highest bidder. Why're you worth so much? I could find out from you, but you'd end up damaged goods. Sorry, I'm not removing the gag. As much as I'd like to, I don't want your answer. Keeps me safe and ready for the next hire."

TT took a call. "On time, no harm. You'll get your precious cargo," he said. "Nope, no alarms went off."

The van bounced wildly in the pauses.

"No worry. The word won't get out, and never will," Talent went on into the phone. "Higher bidders showed, so why no bonus? I didn't violate her. You know where I am? She's got a GPS installed? Thanks for telling me. I'm detouring to rip it out. Why should it hurt her?"

The van stopped. Tanili panicked. She felt TT's rough hands on her neck. He tore her shirt off. "A butcher got to you first," he said. "The implant looks like a pacemaker. If I pull it out will you die? Just nod! What, you don't know? The clients say you have 2 mil in cash. They just told me, said that was my bonus. Where is it?"

He lifted the tape from her lips. "You can have it all if you let me go," she said, struggling.

"I can have it all and 200K besides. What else can you offer?"

"To stay alive. Dead I'm worth nothing to anyone. I can kill myself, and maybe you too, just by thinking," Tanili whispered.

He grabbed at her mouth. She hissed at him then and bit down hard on his fingers and cracked 2 joints.

No sound came from TT for 5 minutes. "I'm going to let you live," he said decidedly. "Cran and Adam are convinced that a gold-based image of you should burnish the Mars space craft. Why?"

"Cran has the patent," Tanili said. "If he's not paying you, who is? Okay, don't tell me. Ruin my image and you'll be bait. The reward will be 5 million."

"If you're right, I'm screwed all ways. That's not happening. Hell, I can't let you go, and I can't keep you. If I hand you over, I'm just an ordinary mercenary villain. If I let you go, you'll finger me. That's not happening either."

"You have a problem," Tanili said, calming.

He pushed her out of the van 3 miles from the CIA HQ gate. "Now, you're tainted," TT said and drove off.

Immediately another car with 2 silent men picked her up.

"**TT HAS LESS** talent than he thinks," Sierra said.

"Give him time to think and his brain short-circuits," Wildcat added. Hearing Futura's blunt voice next, Tanili realized, she was again in the Nebraska lab.

"We can't let Tanili out of our sight for a minute this time," the doc said. "And I won't hire watchers."

"We can't stay here," Patagonia replied, "The press is nosing around now, close to our ground. We have to start appearing, as far away and apart as we can."

"I'll keep her," Jared said, "at least till she's normal."

The 6 laughed together. Tanili would never be herself again. The choice wasn't hers. "I can introduce new tweaks," the doc said. "They may divide her more, but that's the chance we need to take."

Unbound but strapped down, Tanili was free to speak, yet she remained silent. The challenges she'd met had molded her. She longed to repeat the past weeks, for a 2nd chance to break away from her captors. She'd have to disable them first. It would not be jolly. On guard, they didn't trust her. With the speed of ballet, the toe tricks, and unexpected shifts, she could outpace them, but the 6 had rewritten the program in the bean to weird it. Letting her up, they kept leashes on her and sensors. She let her strength build back, by exercising freely in the dark and isometrically in the light.

She tried to generate magnetic heat and kept a firewall around her thoughts. She focused on the chain links. The limits of her mind were few, she found, but she couldn't influence the physical world. She received more than she transmitted. Her moods pulled her off balance. She traveled a pendulum but it stayed in its groove. When she cut loose, she collapsed. Her normal now was a floating stairway to nowhere. Day to day, she imagined her freedom as a low Earth orbit with Cran.

Her mind began to see itself. A network of fine blood vessels lined her skull-wide-sky to trace her life support, to comfort her, to let her believe in her health.

Patagonia's next level up, with a silicon core and grid, had to be death. The end of surprise, the unexpected gone in lie after lie, to a stunted purpose, imposed by the 1st brain, intent on unknowing that life it lost.

Telling Patagonia this, or anything, could only set off a new set of tests. Tanili kept quiet, understanding now, that she was the bridge to a future perhaps not allowed to be built.

The surplus funds from oil and seeds, charity, charm and medical technique would only sabotage itself in time. The 6 had not a clue as to the consequences of what they were doing.

Tanili knew, she could be wrong too, but her gut told her differently: theory lacks the tart flavor of digestion to guide it; that thought is not linear, laddered, or dependent on speech, always. It's many paths at once: architectural, bacterial, individual, communal, easily co-ordinated into a new identity. Sometimes it's just swirls, or a centrifuge of possibilities. Even separated out and tossed off, nothing is wholly pure or impure. Reaching into Patagonia's mind, Tanili learned: liquid 3He is the purest form of matter, without defects or impurities. Yet, sometimes truth is irrelevant, and the transparent, the process, the detours, and the misdirection are the real point.

Tanili dizzied. Cran hovered over her. Was it he? Patagonia twitched. Futura circled. Jared spun into the distance. Wildcat smugged up. Sierra smiled majestically. India lay down on an operating table. Tanili whirled into action, breaking the leather straps. Neck pinching each of the 6 in turn, she fled, leaving them stunned, unable to follow, their minds freezing toward zero.

Tanili danced away from the farmhouse into the distance, then slowed, mindful of her vulnerabilities. After catching her breath, she continued. Within an hour, she was in town, at the bus terminal.

Two wolf-calls away, Cran was waiting with her suitcase.

Cran learned where she was easily. Adept at intercepting radio waves and hard-wired communications, he chose not to. It was simpler to call TT's cousins, Redbud and Glory, who hacked TT directly and traced the doctor paying him, and the other offers in play. The reasons for them weren't evident though. Signals split and bounced in ways suggesting intense federal interest. Naturally confident, but untrained in weapons, Cran decided to pursue Tanili openly. He had every right to, as she had the right to be caught.

Definitely, it seemed that she wanted to be. She clung to him in the bus station, but didn't respond to his questions.

"You have to trust me. I can reward you in 100 ways, and will when no one is chasing. We're in danger from people who think they own me. I've a contract but it's un-enforceable. I can and will walk freely down the street when I'm certain I don't need help, but it's only a matter of time before I do. Then what?"

"Medical help? I went to Stanford. What's wrong with their facilities? It may be expensive, but we'll find a way."

"I've the money. That's not the problem. The probe that's embedded in my neck is. For starters. I think I'd rather talk to Nasa doctors. To them I'll just be a curiosity. I could apply for astronaut training. Nori will help, if you can distract her sister."

"We should fly back."

"No, the bus will give us time to think, and I don't want to risk a pressurized cabin on its way up or down."

Cran and Tanili sat on the hard wooden bench and waited. A Greyhound east would be along in 2 hours. Across from them a man in a bus driver's uniform slumped wearily. "The road is a washboard, slippery without soap, another day in the life of those without hope. I'd rather have my own radio program," he said. "To relate the bits of wisdom I pick up on the way. Every-one has an insight and sometimes an epiphany to convey."

"Start with a daily 3-minute podcast, called *Wisdom*," Cran said. "If you're over your head, you'll know right off. If not, your archive will grow on you and become known to all destinations."

"Thank you for the advice, stranger. I want to better myself. My heritage and my mother insist that I do. You're my first brother in this endeavor."

Cran nodded and turned to Tanili. He wrapped his left arm around her shoulders. Suddenly the man was 2 feet away.

"I've got my own bus, if you're in a rush," he whispered.

"So do we!" Tanili snapped, and jabbed him in the ear with her forefinger.

He fell, rose, and ran off, wobbling, his balance failing.

"He wasn't what he seemed," Tanili said.

Cran was aghast. "That doesn't mean —"

"Yes, it does. Do you see him coming back with the police?"

The worn marble of the station grew cold and gray.

On time, the bus arrived.

Back in Washington, in the garden, Nori laughed at Tanili's request. To become an astronaut, a degree in computing, math, or biology was required, plus 1000 hours of jet pilot time. As ex-military, Nori had that. The government had also paid for her degree. Regardless, it got her nowhere. Tanili needed 10 years or more of hard dedicated work before she could even apply.

"But I'm a special case, with an advantage," Tanili said, "I learn quickly, I work well. No. Well then, I've a 4th brain! It's untested. I've had it less than a year. I might be the subject of a unique emergency grant. I'm a chance to see the future."

"My sister really got to you," Nori said. "She'll continue to put you to the test, I'm sure. Jealousy is her strong suit. You won't win."

"Celestina doesn't know me or want to. You should apply for the grant for me. This is your chance. Once the word gets out, I'll be one big freak show. I'm virgin territory now, more or less. Would you like to talk to the doctor who did it? Cran has her number. He rescued me from her, just by existing."

"I know a good psychiatrist," Nori said.

"You will need one, if I have to insist. I'm the alien you're all seeking," Tanili said. Indeed, eyes were growing inside, against her temples. She dreamed about them over and over, till the lights in her mind blinded her, and she woke wide.

Jolted, Nori was tempted to believe Tanili. Tanili touched her hand, shocking Nori. "I am what I say I am, even if I don't know myself fully. I'm temporary. I won't live. I know that much. Take me to your best doctor, then decide who I am."

The scan showed her brain structure. "It's a uniquely-shaped tumor, benign I would guess. It's not invasive or imposing on adjacent tissue — A biopsy will tell us more," the doctor said in his home office.

Tanili upped and left. Nori followed. "The biopsy will only show weird brain tissue. I'll be sent for more scans, biopsies, and invasive probes, without clothes," Tanili said. "For a Nasa doctor, I'll do that, okay? Arrange it. May I stay with you?"

Nori's house with its guest cells was near-perfect. Waiting to be examined by Nasa, Tanili became the hive's natural center. Adam drew too much attention with his pamphlets though. The press circled him, sometimes knocking at the door. He makes a good story. His Bentley has no reverse. He doesn't retreat, even en route to his newest heart of darkness. He persists in saying that we lost a generation to cannibals, but that jungle choice is good and should not be buried by civil law, that the future discounts the past, that those who identify with failure become failures themselves, that hypocrisy is an unpeelable hard varnish. In fact, his leaflets are censored, trashed, and popular. He lives as he wants and says as he chooses. That people take him so seriously amazes him; that they think he's always angry and ready to fight unsettles him. Mostly he floats in his own haze, maintains a fine balance, and judges intuitively. He understands Tanili best in his way and encourages her. He wants her near and says so. He only regrets that whatever he chronicles now can not be released. Yet, he's sure, someone already hears him. It's possible. Speeding near home, he crushed a Tesla, driven by a Chinese national with a Korean physicist as a passenger. Fenders bent, Adam's car still takes him to Whole Foods, the White House, and Home Depot. The back wheel wobbles and may soon fall off, but Adam seems to have charmed the fates. He smirks at danger. Tanili has begun to smile with him.

His more serious enemy, the Russians, bounce off his firewalls. Sooner or later their coders will hack in, but Tanili is his only secret. In any case, the brick house next door belonging to a Marine general is a mini-fort and arsenal.

Cran is the trouble. Tanili fascinates him more than ever, but Celestina trips him at every turn. She's the reverse of what she seems. Her pose of an art to everything and a science to none is enticing, intuitive, and fun, but she's alone in effect.

Her sister, Nori, is the opposite: direct, assertive, consistent. She's taken to teaching Tanili, giving her the grounding she needs to become an astronaut from the start.

Weeks on, news from North Dakota shocked the networks. The police found a farm house of horrors, a graveyard of failed human experiments, and no one to charge. *The Daily Mail,* a British paper, published photos. Only the number of deaths was exaggerated. Baboons, long dead, far from their original home, with holes drilled in the sides of their heads and other craven abuses, filled cages labeled Shame, Harass, Threaten, Blame, Cry, and Curse, as if with plagues. To add to the gruesome imagery, torn-off limbs with added fingers, double-muscling, claws, suckers, teeth, beaks, and shredders were also found, rotting in an unplugged refrigerator. The farm belonged to local doctors, unavailable for interviews, for obvious reasons. No clues to their whereabouts were evident, or ever would be.

A national debate followed over whether the universe was broken, now and forever. New theories dominated about DNA conspiracies, condemning and dismissing all possibilities at once. At one extreme, some half-wits believed it's impossible to improve a brain or create intelligence, and that race is a myth because it's not in the DNA, and like all myths, its origin is lost in time and just a literary construct. Layered on top of this theme was the belief, we should implant DNA filters to prevent Caucasians from even thinking they're white or any other color. The absurd made sense to the diminished, of course. Double-speak became the order of the day, with true science nowhere to be found. If Tanili could choose she'd allow all speculations.

Adam collaborated on a book called *Searching for Science*, meanwhile, but it didn't change a thing. Nasa had asked his clan for slogans to inspire an ecological mind-set. They were making that part of their mission, to insist that science defined life, and that eco-tech is our best tool for fruitful living.

Immediately, Tanili officially dropped to deep secret, not to be revealed, ever, whatever the necessity. Nasa could no longer admit she existed. Even to Cran, she grew invisible. The key consequence: Tanili lost access to generous medical treatment. The worm, intensely disagreeable as ever, stayed in place. Tanili thought quietly about dying.

Day by day, death was her one and only truism.

She woke from a bad dream, overwhelmed, candy-colored circles of light rolling in her eye, wanting her to stare at them in awe and wonder, but she knew she'd be stressing her retina more, as the light-circles tugged from the opposite direction, before her lens reversed them. She resisted, froze in place, and her panic passed. Her sight returned to normal, but she'd seen inside herself. That she could do so terrified her.

She often thought of herself as a dead woman walking now. Her poison was already ingested. Cran would not be her last meal. Her hands trembled slightly. Her joints ached. Her breath was a squeal and a rattle. Her knees often buckled. She'd be her own executioner, she knew.

She fought back. It did no good. She imagined Patagonia saying, 'Tanili's like a black hole that's lost its charge, that has mass and spin and emits radiation, but has no light at all.'

It was the bug talking. Tanili struggled against it. Her symptoms lessened. Nori offered to help.

By enrolling Tanili into a pre-med program, Nori opened the door to the astronaut process for Tanili. Adam insisted that a Pandora's box would burst instead, within a year.

Tanili absorbed herself in her studies. A quick learner, she now woke up right-clicking a mouse, though her hand was empty. In 6 months, she'd finished 2 years work and applied for medical school. Adam quizzed her when she asked him to. In turn he asked Tanili to help clarify his excess complexity, and turn around his reversals, when he lost direction.

"The wheeling life and the eeling fife stay peaceful, now that vines in the sunset send shivers down my squidly spine," Adam said, "Do you get my drift?"

"Just the rhythm. Does anything else matter? I feel your reach. It's fun enough. Don't try to do more," Tanili answered.

"Thanks, but sometimes, I want to mean what I say. To shock the marrow into producing new blood. I've a task now shaping a Scotsman who could be the next Swift, but he's not sardonic enough. I can rewrite him to be. Here. Dance is dear to you. Listen to this: 'Censors enter at intermission, to arrest the weak German nouns masquerading as women, while toe-twirling and wearing edible gold leaf. Yah, comedy is falling afoul of speech laws in the farterland today.'"

"I don't understand," Tanili said.

"Sinistergrams thin to sinister greats," Adam said.

He doubled over laughing, his hand covering his mouth as if not to share his infectious state. Perhaps it was to hide his cracked front teeth. Tanili smiled. She couldn't help herself. Adam the lifter lightened her mind. Adam the argument, however, denied everyone. She sensed that she'd have fallen in love with him otherwise, as Cran was distant again. He came and went at Celestina's bidding.

Tanili u-turned to learn from her too. Celestina's grace was in her face, her charm in her tone of voice. Susceptible to her flutterings, Adam denied himself, and her flirtations in turn focused on Cran, naive soul that he was, unaware that she had spent college summers pasting doll's eyes on fish to make them look fresh in a market stall, that she'd next served clear soup in stiletto heels to gourmands in Washington, and experimented with onion ice cream, to break down the cholesterol ingested, before she happened on synthetic chlorophyl for her lotions and potions kit. An eco-princess purveying favors, enticing all farmer's markets, she didn't have to out-think her audiences, just offer up her counter.

Two semesters later, Tanili felt real again. She understood not only her own chemistry but Celestina's now.

"I'm an illegal alien in name only," Tanili told Nori, "And I'll have my revenge on those who made me without caring. I'm glad you sponsored me, and hid me. I'll repay you, promise. I'll also alter the club of 6 and not involve you."

Tanili had learned how to make any protein water-soluble, so that a person might drown in his own dissolving. Very nasty business that, but inevitable, if need be.

Meanwhile, she practiced her swagger privately, as public dancing meant special attention and interview questions.

With Celestina, Tanili made hasty pudding, sad bread, and corn-cob candles for venison dinners that Adam unfroze from past hunting trips. Tensions under the table were equal to those above it, as Celestina rubbed thighs with every new guest, while the dinner itself redefined the daily quest.

"Get the magic out of the myth, and I'll agree," Nori liked to say. "And always remember, we're masters of our own universe, no one has a claim on us."

"Yes, dear," Adam always answered, "Really, I like your rules, now that the Wild West is back."

"And who are we hanging today?" Celestina asked sweetly.

"That hang-dog sheriff who looks like death," Adam said. "He'd be my pick. What say, how about Redbud? He was your favorite tormenter once. He'll be at dinner."

Redbud Bjorki had chaperoned his daughter Susu to DC on a school trip, but he had ulterior motives. He owned forests north of San Francisco, near the Oregon border, and wanted fire-prevention funding to clear the overgrowth, along with permission to thin the oldest redwoods for his sawmills. Then too, he intended to put in a bid for the burls in adjacent federal forests, to sell to art carvers. He'd hired Adam to write the grant proposal and do the auction bidding. Redbud's presence raised the price while Adam's lowered it at most fine auctions.

"My renegade days are past," Redbud said. "I've got security clearance and a daughter. Law enforcement can hang itself."

"The ideals are gone, are they?" Adam asked.

"Big sister doesn't give a man a chance," Redbud said.

"Cel-well-sister is offering," Nori said.

Celestina threw the chocolate mousse pie, that Redbud had brought, at Nori, and missed. "The mop's in the pantry," Nori said smugly. "And pay back Redbud for his lost luscious pie."

Tanili listened amused. She didn't pick up on many of the references, but she got the gist. Dinner conversation was only entertainment anyway. Shadow plots against darker federal agencies lit up the table play. The underlying theme in every case was always, let us walk free and we won't break your knees.

Over time, Tanili also fed on the dinner thinking. It filled her brain, never fully, but she linked her class chemistry to novel possibilities. No one questioned her. Guests intuitively knew what they hadn't been told, and were smart enough not to ask what they weren't meant to know.

Most clients saw Adam's resources as crucial to their success. His newest card said 1 ACROSS. A 2nd read EMPTY HOLSTERS, always good for a grin.

In due course, Tanili sensed a joke before it was told, and her glow of good health lifted all who met her. She gave a suitcase full of cash to Nori, in appreciation. It wasn't examined or questioned.

AFTER 2 YEARS more of coursework Tanili celebrated her 21st birthday. Adam gave her a deep-red manzanita burl, carved into a bowl ridged like a brain. "To have and to hold whatever the future brings," he said.

She wrote to her parents then and her uncle and aunt. "I'm surprisingly well, but it'll be a while before you see me again. You may not recognize me. I hardly recognize myself. Please, if my ex-husband asks, say you never hear from me, either. I will bring back the moon and the stars and make you proud."

She wanted to add, that if they ever needed medical help, she would be there for them but omitted a return address on the flowery envelope.

Cran went absent then. Celestina too. She headed off to sell New York to itself with envy soaps, and suck-up suds, dry airs, and wee trumpets of change. Creamy hypocrisy, 12 crotch monkey pots and a perfume called FAILURE ISN'T AN OPTION filled her sample case. She earned enough for a pimp's new El Dorado and cruised Park Avenue with the top down and her thumbs up to the losers for a week before coming home, still as restless and flirtatious as ever, though the car never left the driveway again.

The household thrived, rented a beehive, and harvested 70 pounds of honey that summer. The bees swarmed around Tanili, to greet and feed their new queen, it seemed. When she backed away, blushing, none followed.

"Beware, wasps will sting a queen to death," Celestina said at dinner.

"Practice make you imperfect," Adam said to her.

"We're all equal," Nori answered.

"What's so great about equality?" Adam asked. "It's boring, burdensome and bullshit, not in the least real. Equal rights and opportunity, sure, but for each, value must be achieved, not a given. We can't take brains from one to give to another. Or weight or size. Perhaps we should, but there's equal reason not to. We're not reversing evolution, if I'm captain or king."

"Are you running for office?" Nori asked.

"Hell, no, I just like to hear myself talk."

"You could fool me," Nori said. "Your fans are waiting for a new manifesto to lead them."

"I'm sure they'd prefer a real mutation," Tanili said.

In the ensuing thoughtful silence, Celestina wove Tanili's braids into a wreath around her head and smiled in delight.

"Am I just a doll to you?" Tanili asked.

"I wish you were."

"I don't. It's lonely being me," Tanili answered simply.

That night the group of 6 visited, as if they'd been invited. The bean brought them. Like threads unweaving, they argued in tangles. They'd lost Tanili completely, they knew. They could not openly snatch her, offer rewards, or hire outside help. They'd be betrayed in 2 seconds. Besides, a gauntlet awaited. New laws had passed. The national debate still raged. People inflamed by the recent news blamed the big state and choked bitterly, but the dark and the light like to fight, and fashion pardons itself. Nothing changed, but small show downs allowed for smart wins in the flanks. The 6 paid their respects to Tanili and ruefully left.

At the Nebraska farm, the 6 still gathered monthly, in dread of ongoing failure, as if they'd already triggered defeat in all directions. Wildcat wondered what it'd be like if he'd never knew a perfect woman: the firm supple flesh under billowing pants, the pleasure on her face in a casual breeze, the aware smile without irony.

Sierra, to cure herself, planned to run 1,000 marathons in 1,000 days on the road to enlightenment.

Jared intended to seed and reseed himself, rather than be crippled by increasingly volatile blood pressure and involuntary intentional shaking, that neither pills or exercise could calm.

India chose the irrational for her remedy. Logic told her: men are born with aggressive instincts, and as all aggression is abusive, all men are abusive and should be punished at birth.

The doctor also went weird, believing that women are killed in disproportionate to men, so soon there'll be no women left.

Patagonia kept her own council.

Tanili decided again on who in the club she'd liquify and spray on a canvas, yet in her 4 brains she remained of 2 minds about everything, though she'd re-found her sense of balance.

"Abolish ICE, but freeZE them all," Wildcat insisted.

"Hiss at his PMS world," India answered.

Sierra peaked with platitudes about ugly women politics.

Futura sneered and returned to her laboratory.

Singly the 6 were fragmenting, and their league as well.

Tanili largely disconnected from them. She wished she were a baby again, born without fear into a welcoming world and growing to command the unknown as she pleased. She had accepted the role of guinea pig instead and now suffered the down-side. Not really though. Her discomforts were negligible. She was free to become a new person. Her life was larger than she imagined. In her mind, at least.

After acing her coursework and skipping ahead, with a pre-med degree in sight, Tanili enrolled in flight school, to qualify for the astronaut application. She'd need 1000 hours piloting a jet. She still had the funds. The Carolinas might be quicker, but she picked California to learn, as Cran was now at Stanford heading toward a PhD in Invention, a program he created for himself. Find the best principles for the quickest way forward included reversing direction, starting from scratch, being the rebel, and engaging in creative chaos, but zig-zagging a direct line was his favorite weave for the million dollar prizes that Nasa offered. Apart from accidents, luck, and imagination, finding the most straight-forward path worked best, simply.

Yet for Cran, Tanili was a maze without an entrance or exit. Worse, his fears restricted his longing for her. Her unknowns constricted him further. He was sure that he couldn't handle them. The possibility of pain pre-echoed sharply. His father, who ran toward danger, was a crippling lesson. He needed crutches all the time now.

Tanili had her own ambivalences. Studying, flying hours, and acing exams weren't enough. Becoming a test pilot was more meaningful. For an astronaut, surviving experimental aircraft was the top training. But it was daunting, not a dance, perhaps dimensions beyond her, electronic in a 5th brain way. What'd happen if she quit half-through the program?

She couldn't. Becoming an astronaut now meant freeing her brain.

The bean tree phone in her neck was the obstacle. With practice, she'd learnt how to turn it on and off at will. Yet Jared and Patagonia were useful. Perhaps Cran could save them, by reprogramming the bean, or scrambling its frequencies, to reach them?

Cran's plan though was for a dozen start-up companies.

"Upstart companies," he said, "We're functional and running already. None need more than a drawer. The products are ready."

Tanili smiled. His head was nearly as swollen as hers.

Of necessity, in fact, she wore a head-shaping helmet now, to keep her appearance normal. Her skull bones still hadn't fully hardened and were pushing outward as her 4th brain kept growing. No doubt, Cran saw her as a freak. Strangers thought she belonged to an unidentified motorcycle gang. She asked a doctor for treatment. He refused. "Nature takes care of itself," he said, "Yours has an extended schedule, that's all."

She accepted this. Her bones were nearly fused. She'd only need the helmet for 6 months more. Meanwhile, when asked to remove it, she professed to a life-threatening injury and had a doctor's note to prove it. TSA was dubious. The beat cop and local traffic police as well.

TANILI SAT ALONE on a hard plastic chair in the waiting area at Dulles. Her awareness floated above her, not connected to any part of her physical being, beyond the high ceiling and into the flight paths approaching the runways. She heard control tower voices, unclear but constant, droning in a staccato rhythm.

On the 1st leg of her San Francisco connection, she listened to the pilot mumbling about his investments. The stewardess, with her V-shaped face and pointed-toe pixie shoes, stared at her strangely. Wheels up to wheels down took 3 hours.

Tanili deplaned in Dallas and flew back to DC.

There the voice of Futura rang in her ears. Every doctor was Futura to her now. Yet she needed someone. Her brain was leaking. She shouldn't have flown, even in a pressurized cabin. "We can bleed your brain," Adam said.

"I have to give up my dreams. Will you give me new ones?"

"Would that I could," Adam said pacing the rug in figure 8s.

"I've begun to see people moving in slow motion."

"Is your clock speeding up, or your mind relaxing?"

"To dock at the space station, the shuttle has to slow to 2" per second," Tanili said, "Nori taught me that."

"She left something out then. Deliberately, I suspect. The rocket always knows where it is and where it should be. It can adjust itself autonomously. Humans are only systems monitors, test pilots aren't needed anymore, awareness training is key."

"I see, California was a mistake. Good, I'd rather be here, if I may. I've found my community. I don't want to be on my own. Cran doesn't have time for me there, it seems."

Tanili stretched out on the corduroy couch and closed her eyes. Adam talked on soothingly, openly speculating. "I'm not trying to mow the Great Plains, or start a wild fire in the cities, but I could with your help. With the generous expenses you gave Nori and me, we could start a political home party around you. The free-lance vigilantes are wanting my hide. The knee-jerks too. Sheep in wolves' clothing. The creed of greed is at work."

"Am I your mascot then?" Tanili asked, her eyes still shut.

"Well, no, we can't admit you exist either. You're inspiration. Just knowing that you exist allows me to say, that the Bezos' Machine is all sluices and suds, that the *New York Times* has a 1/4 bill feed from Mexico's fat Mr. Slim. And, *CNN* is the new Confederacy of Numb-Numbs. But opposition and truth are bad planks in a party platform. We'd fall through."

"Is inspiration all you want from me?" Tanili said, sitting up.

"Is it not enough, or too much?" Adam asked.

"Every other man wants more. Why don't you desire me? You're not even ambivalent. Your wife and you have completely different rhythms. You may resonate together, but you're self-canceling, really. Adam Q, Nori Nuuk don't pair. Yet, you seem perfectly content."

"What's wrong with comfortable?"

"You worship her mind, and she's amused by your random perversity and quickness, but you're not complimentary."

"Has she said so? How do you know?"

"Celestina tempts you, but I don't."

"Ah, but she's Nori inside out."

"And I?"

"Am still evolving. I see more clearly, when not caring."

"You're on track then and know it," Tanili said, leaning back and closing her eyes again, sinking deeply into the couch. "If I can't live in the air, I will underwater."

"As an amphibian or an alien?"

"One and the same. My creators wanted to cripple me, as a mermaid. I needed to swim free. I can go back to them and ask for help, but I'd be deceiving myself to think they'd release me."

"What do we do about your leaking, meanwhile?"

"I'll prevail."

"Then stay here. We'll improvise a future together."

"I wouldn't survive a spin-flip sub-harmonic," Tanili said. "Oh! Sorry, that's Patagonia talking through me."

But it was Jared she heard next. "I could buy time on the space station to print organs to replace mine. They'd grow in 3 dimensions there rather than 2, as in a petri dish here."

Jared sounded very sick. Tanili sympathized. His breath gone, he'd lost his good health. Genetic manipulations or even new stents in his arteries, wouldn't heal him, after the fact, even at the cost of all his wealth. He wondered aloud if he'd picked up something from Futura, by way of contamination, deliberately or not. Tanili had nothing to offer, to prop him up. He disappeared.

Celestina joined Tanili and Adam, with a new catalog for her company's wares; it included masks, waters, scrubs, muds, washes, and ointments. She taunted Tanili: "A knife is quicker."

"You selling that as a sticker?" Tanili asked.

"You're lucky you didn't go to San Francisco. The fog is 2-toned, red from the fires and gray with ash. The cities downwind from the forests burning. You should know, Cran may come back, to get you. His thesis was rejected. If he includes you, if he claims to have invented you, he'll need to prove..."

"Not happening."

"I told him. That you'd also love to tie him up and tickle his dick, but I might kill you both when you're done."

"You're so out of line, sister-in-law," Adam said, "A lip up is the most you'll achieve, by your kind of provoking."

"That's harsh," Celestina said, "I was just having fun, and being real, if you get my drift. By the way, a man named Frick wants to see you. He's at the front door. I told him, no visitors today. He said he'll wait, however long it takes. He's dressed slick, but he looks black-ops to me."

"I'll have the general deal with him," Adam said. "Listen, sister, make it clear. Nothing's here for anyone. No butterflies drinking from a bird's eye. No ghosts to extort. And no lives lost waiting to be found. Tanili's sponsors know now, the financial benefits they'd imagined can't be realized; they can't parade Tanili publicly; she can't endorse any of their endeavors. Not now or ever. She can't appear out of nowhere, as ambassador of a new way. During our lifetime, she'll always be an alien. Well, at least for a decade."

"Frick didn't mention her. He just wants you."

"Damn, I'll be borrowing the general's guns next. The one that shoots sideways, around corners, is my favorite."

"I have a better hat trick," Celestina said. "Tanili's sponsors should have thought of it. Using a transparent aerogel with 99% porosity, to contain and shape her brain. It works with skin moisturizer. Why not DNA and nerve juice?"

"Too late there," Tanili said, intrigued. "My new sponsors live here now and you're one of them, like it or not."

"That's even harsher," Celestina said. "You know, I'm not supposed to say, but my company transplanted a few brains in its time, and found out that certain grouplings will not accept a 4th brain. It gives them a persistent headache. I can't tell you more. My boyfriends were sworn to secrecy."

Adam knew, Celestina with her agility would surround him. He left her to plot with Tanili and went by way of the backyard to the general's mini-mansion next door. Tanili followed ten steps back, to watch. The general, with his 2-star helmet on, sat on his power mower, sneering at his hydrangea.

"I've come to borrow a Glock, if you've extra," Adam said.

"You've got new women to protect?" he asked.

"No, it's for me, I've got a guy named Frick at my door."

"Franklin Frick? Sharp, stone-faced, a smiling cobra. Send him here."

"A buddy of yours, is he? I'd still like a weapon."

"To protect yourself from me? Or him? Okay, I'll bite, if I get a share of the low-hanging fruit."

"Your wife might squash in above you. Last I saw her, she was a head taller."

"Only when she's not on her knees."

"Not nice," Adam said, "Do you have an extra Glock or two?"

"You shouldn't have a gun, boy. If you've got both weapons

and words, you'll get busted. Stick to the words. They aren't illegal. You can wave them as much as you want, even drunk in a bar, and you're cool. Leave the guns to me. If you're worried about Frick, don't. His command can't touch mine."

"Suppose I just keep the gun in the house and never take it out. I've trained myself. No worry."

"Okay. Done. I've got a box of teflon-coated ammo for you too. Won't leave blood-stains on your wall-paper."

"Should I be looking forward to a home invasion?"

The general filled Adam's request to the letter and gave him a remote besides. "Learn the key code, and you're cool. The red button is me. Hit it and I'll be there. It's an honor to serve. As long as you stick to rocket science, I'm with you."

Adam kept Frick waiting another 3 hours. He seemed unfazed when Adam snapped open the door, wearing a shoulder holster. Expressionless, Frick pitched an absurd rationale for access to Adam's property. "The Congressional budget wars are shutting down the government tomorrow. National forests have to close too. No camping on federal property will be allowed. Anyone already there will be kicked off. You have a private unmonitored entrance behind your house. I'll pay you, as gate-keeper —"

"Nice try. Give the general next door a shot. He likes you."

"Risky. Negative associations," Frick said, "He's too loose a canon. When he shoots himself, I'll not be in the way."

"That's odd to hear. He's opinionated yes, a loyal neighbor too. The evidence speaks for itself. Clear enough?"

"Your best interest coincides with a national and astronomical fate. I can sanction anything, even kidnapping, you realize. Do I make myself clear too?"

"As bullet-proof glass. But I've got .50 calibre hollow-points now that love to explode."

"That's cool. Tell me, what's so great about science?"

"It's self-policing.

"That's a thought," Frick said, "I'll take that with me."

NORI had conniptions. "Adam! You can't just say what comes into your head! Even the general warned you!"

Adam wasn't listening. He'd been taught by his mother to fight and be willing to lose. "Bravery is half the battle," she still said at every dream-visit. Besides, Adam didn't sense danger from Fitch. To the contrary, Fitch was willing to do anything to be part of the action around Tanili, but he couldn't be trusted. His resources made him dangerously unpredictable, and Tanili could not counter that.

"Nori's right. Fitch doesn't know his own strength," Tanili said, "just as I don't understand my own mind, yet."

"We can put it to the test," Celestina said.

"Bad idea," Nori said, "No, it's a good idea, but pre-mature. Right now, we can't fight the world, or even fend it off, without friends to back us up. Having a political party on call'd help."

"Ah, but the Democrats want to destroy democracy, and the Republicans to fracture the republic even more, or is it vice versa? Either way, we've no allies. We need our own party. And organizing Adam's fans would be the best start," Tanili said.

"Whoa! Hold on, all of you," Adam said. "A club, a creed, a neo-tribal brotherhood, a sisterhood, a hive, a cult, a quorum, a guild, with firewalls around ourselves, with no goal but to have what's denied us in our public existence, that's all I want. And that's enough. We're on the ground, the same ground. The space station should be our base. We could be regrowing Tanili's brain without gravity, refining it, removing impurities, or adding them, as needed. Nasa is the natural partner, but can't be now knowingly. Private companies have no constraint, little over-sight, and are an indulgence to folks who want a new body. They don't think to want a new brain."

"I'm with you," Tanili said.

"I'm not," Nori said, "I still work for Nasa."

"And I won't be left alone, to lose," Celestina said.

A week later Nori wheeled in a drum-shaped model satellite once used for practice and hung it, with its broken antenna and burned tiles, from the living room ceiling, where it spun freely, ominously, and ghost-like. Tanili saw it as her tumbling mind and stared at the small suspended drum-sat endlessly.

She could slow it down and speed it up at will. The spin rate didn't change, only her perception of it. She drove a car the same way now. At dangerous corners, she foresaw collisions, and in slow motion perceived how to avoid them. Her reactions were quicker as a result. Accidents didn't happen. Anticipating, she timed her responses perfectly. She could hear other drivers as they neared, cursing and flinching in fear, when she played the encounter too closely. Her control gave her new confidence. She saw every second and seized it.

Adam and Nori noticed the difference. Tanili decided to improve on it. "Let's hire a private satellite company, who uses expansion modules to launch cube-sats, to experiment with my brain, no questions asked," Tanili said.

"But we don't know what we're doing," Nori protested.

"We don't need to," Adam answered, "We just take a sample from you and another from Tanili, culture them in space, and do a DNA and spectrographic analysis on return. No one else is the wiser."

"We still don't know what we're doing," Nori insisted.

"Tanili will interpret the results for us. She's had 2 years of pre-med training."

Tanili liked the idea.

"We can send you into Earth space after all," Nori said.

"I guess this means, we've adopted you," Adam said.

They bought 200K of used analytical equipment, meant for biological monitoring, from a nearby medical school and, in the basement of the house, set up a lab, not nearly as complete as Dr. Futura's, but for the next phase of analysis and testing it served well.

Hiring a satellite company wasn't as simple. The cost was

69

prohibitive, but empty space was better filled and Adam offered to do PR for the company, when the "truth can be told," he said. "Mind you, for now I can't give you a hint of anything else."

"As long as you carry liability insurance, we don't care what you cram in your cube-sat. We wouldn't know the difference anyway. Unless it came back dead," the bow-tied salesman said.

"If we grow an extra brain, we'll give you one," Adam joked with a wink. That satisfied the nerd-weird man.

Cran meanwhile came back to claim the proof he needed for his thesis, but Celestina threw him out. Adam invited him back, for his mechanical skill, to build the cube-sat.

Cran worked in Adam's book-lined study. The cube-sat was the size of a bread box with a toaster inside. Its unfolded solar-panel skirt reminded Tanili of a tutu. She painted white ballet shoes on the bottom surface of the cube-sat, and signed her name. Having claimed the cube's identity, she took samples from herself, and Nori, Celestina, and Adam as well to ride into space, fed by nutrient gels and slurries and aerogels. Only the leakage from Tanili's brain was included though.

She wanted to remove the bean at the top of her spine and send it off also, but decided that it'd be better alone, and as such, belonged on a second trip, pending the success of the first.

The club of 6 meanwhile debated whether to start all over again with someone else or renew its efforts to recover Tanili. This was hardly a choice. If they chased Tanili, they'd be caught. They could begin again, but they were unsure what to do differently. Jared volunteered himself. Futura rejected him. She only wanted a near perfect specimen, who hadn't shown exceptional ability yet. Jared argued that Einstein would've been the best subject, but Jared himself was as close as the club was going to get. She wanted TT, to punish him for letting Tanili get away in the 1st place. The argument was unresolved. Tanili tried to enter her vote, to break the stalemate, but getting transmissions was far easier than sending them. The club of 6 was in flux.

Nora, Celestina, Cran, Adam and the general attended the

cube-sat's desert blast-off. Nevada was too far for Tanili to fly and too dangerous. The trip was a costly indulgence, but each of the group had a part of themselves to wave to. Except for the general. He didn't know why he was wanted, only that he was safe-guarding the future somehow, but he was in his element. His opinions had a welcoming audience at the incubator space-port. Support for a local chapter of a futurist party was evident, especially if fed by a Filipino cook and her banana ketchup for fried bass, indigenous elsewhere.

"What we need is to depopulate the Earth," the general said. "It's a no-brainer. You guys have the science here to do it. It'd be so easy. You don't even need me."

The local-brain-trust seemed to take him seriously.

Cran set up a live feed for Tanili. She was numb with excitement. The count-down clock froze at 3.

"It's a do-over," Cran told her. "Not to worry. The ice won't melt till it's warmed in space. The probes and sensors are on continuous send."

And indeed, the 2nd countdown 2 hours later ended in the roar of the rocket as it slowly lifted off. The tethers fell away, the rocket picked up speed and arched into the stratosphere within minutes, separating along the way, and releasing the cube-sats to their final orbit. Hope drifted with the smoke trail beyond the limits of sight.

In DC, Tanili sighed in relief and danced deliriously around the screen. In the silence, pausing after a run across the room, she heard glass breaking. Brief, sharp, and coming from the backdoor, it signalled an intruder. She grabbed the Glock from the desk drawer and locked herself in the basement. The wood door shuddered as someone hammered the handle off. Tanili fired 3 shots through the door panels. She heard a groan, quick steps, and quiet. After 5 minutes she emerged from the basement to explore. A brief trail of blood stopped short before reaching the back door. Tanili spun heal and toe ready to shoot again, but found no one, and the damage minor. She didn't call the police, as she'd have to explain herself. Instead she gathered blood samples and froze them along with the door handle.

Aware that anyone with skill could listen in, Tanili waited for the group to return to relate the event in person.

Cran searched outside and found cylinders of oxygen and nitrous oxide abandoned in the herb garden. Nori wanted to phone the police. Adam stopped her. "They'll be back weekly," he said, "and for all we know, one of them was the intruder."

"Agreed, we don't need the press," Nori said.

The incident was shelved, till the blood samples revealed a rare bone disease and random mutations. Tanili refrigerated it to save for the next satellite launch. Nori took samples meanwhile, from each layer of the bean. The blood matched the top layer. The intruder was one of the 6 then, but which one?

It had to be Jared. Why? What changed? Had Dr. Futura poisoned his seeds? With his unknowing help?

Tanili, all the more determined now, the consequences be damned planned to extract the bean somehow. For the 1st time, it hadn't warned her.

"Is something wrong?" Adam asked.

"Yes. Why do you have more flexibility with 3 brains than I have with 4?"

"I'm not in danger. I can laugh at myself. I've nothing to lose. And I don't care about consequences. I'm playing. Everything is fair game. Is that enough?" Adam asked.

"You're a floating bubble of indifference to everything you touch?"

"On many levels, no. On others, yes."

"That's creepy. Is there an elevator in your consciousness?"

"Yes. A space elevator, to take me up to the satellites."

"Can I do my thinking there, as your guest?"

"That might be dangerous, or even deadly. You have to discover your destructive side and learn to work with it first."

"You mean, I should kill my tormentors? I think so too."

CRAN FLUSHED, embarrassed that he had to admit significant failure for the 1st time. Still living as a student, held back from the world of adult importance, redoing his thesis, diminished him, disappointing his expectations for himself. There had to be a better way forward. Indeed, hanging with Tanili to help her, firmed up his confidence, gave him a sense that he'd fill the sky as his father had, with a retrospective photographic show at the Smithsonian one day, but differently.

He confessed this to Tanili. She laughed. "So then, if I'm stuffed and exhibited at the American History branch of the Smithsonian you'll be happy with yourself? You do know that you didn't create me, save me, fulfill me, or allow me to realize my own potential? You chose Celestina."

"Well, yes, by twisted choice," Cran said. "She offered herself, completely. What can I say? I inherited my bad manners from my dad, my mom says, it's in my genes."

"Not funny. Sad, really. You joke, but my brain's on trial. Real errors may be embedded. If you fixated on me, you'd play The 4th Mind Game; object: brain-gain; format: board-game. You'd have a best-seller and your thesis, a creation resulting from your rules, lived by experience. You thought that, having invented 4-color gold printing, you'd succeed intuitively ever after. But denying me, you wronged me. And you'll do it again. I can run circles around you, if I choose, if I felt comfortable with myself, but I'm aware of all the unknowns that I'm living with. With Nori's help, and Adam's guidance, I've acquired tools, and the knowledge to be myself. I thought I loved you once."

"Sorry. I'm really sorry. I made a true mistake," Cran said. "I didn't intend to —" He stopped, noticing Celestina hovering in the doorway, holding back, not rushing forth to compete.

"You're brilliant," Celestina said to Tanili. "I can learn from you too, but I have little to offer in return."

"If I knew all the factors, Tanili," Cran said, "the variables

Futura considered, I could make you into an app at the least, and at best a theoretical model. I wish I could speak to her."

"You can. Offer yourself. You'll learn more than you want, and you'll live it. The only way forward is by trial and error. Rules only get in the way."

"I'm a coward," Cran said.

"That's a fair statement," Celestina said, "You didn't leap to defend me either. Are you so easily seduced? Not all men are!"

"I'll never win this one," Cran said, sinking into a seat.

"You thought you would?" both Tanili and Celestina asked at once.

Cran was smart enough not to respond. "I won't be a student forever," he finally said. "Can I get another chance?"

"To do what?"

"Whatever you offer me. Both of you."

"Clever boy," Celestina said, "Too bad, you're too late. We're not even either-or anymore."

Cran wanted to sink further, under the couch and through the floor, but sensed that if he took his punishment now, he'd be rewarded later.

And so he was. Tanili and Celestina let him off the hook, by sending him next door, to receive quick-draw lessons in the general's sub-basement shooting range. "The women will make a real man of you yet," the general said.

Cran grimaced.

"Okay, so what's going on over there, that I'm not supposed to know?" the general asked.

"The women are beyond gourmet kitchen chemistry, but they're not goddesses yet," Cran said and put three bullets into the target bull's eye.

"Good job. Quick learner. Tell me, how do we get Adam off his ass and into the fray?"

"You can't. Political confrontation just isn't his way. He's a brainiac. Let him be."

"Not my style, son. He's what we need. You know the Marine

74

saying about when you hear gunfire, you run towards it not away? Otherwise you're just going to die tired?"

"Except Adam's not a Marine."

"We're all Marines, boy, and don't forget that!"

"Even the president?"

"Especially the president! Even the wimpy ones with wart-less women. It's my job to stand in, pop all blisters. Got that? Adam's a special category. He's got the guidance about him, you can see it easily. Tanili too. She's got a thing about her, even quiet. She's a rare bird. You almost never see her kind."

Cran returned to Tanili and told her, "The general thinks you've something of the divine about you. Hoist a starred flag and he'll follow you into battle anywhere."

"I hope not," Tanili said, "No, I hope you've learned more than that. Do you still want Futura's records?"

"I'll take whatever I can get."

"Then go, take them, one way or another, but keep in mind, her lab is as wired as an electric chair."

Cran filled a back-pack and flew to Nebraska, knowing that he'd be allowed back burned, but not empty-handed.

Redbud, the young, retired eco-terrorist and rich, lumber mill owner, returned, looking for Cran.

"You just missed him," Adam said, "but hang around. The general next door wants a wood shop. Set him up. Involuntary retirement isn't far off for him. Whatever your cost, I'll pay for it. It's time to build an ark."

"You're putting me on."

Adam put 20K on the table.

Redbud started on the project immediately. 30K more and it was done within a week, with sawdust vacuums in place under the best band saws, sanding tables, lathes, joiners and routers. The cost in fact was far higher than Adam paid, but Redbud thought of the workshop as his too, available for use 24 hours a day. It filled the walkout basement at the general's.

Tanili guessed that the wood shop would see military use

75

before long. Meanwhile she pressed Adam on his plans and considered one for herself: Switzerland made the most sense for an expert removal of the bean. And so it happened.

She insisted on going on her own.

Celestina left also, on a sales trip to the West Coast.

With the other women gone, Nori wore her 5 carat wedding ring again. Adam realized, she too had renewed plans for him.

He used the wood shop to create a survival pen. The clip could kill, the flint cap light fires, and the dark ink still flowed beautifully. He then bought Kevlar gloves with steel threads woven in. His horizons widened. His new sphere of influence, the spread of his clan, excited his awareness of dimension. Distance no longer mattered. Just as Israeli drone operations ran well from Scottdale, Arizona, and Tanili could at moments see beyond the mountain tops, Adam also began to feel the range of his power.

Nori had been at the US facility in the UK and come away impressed with its operational reach. Suddenly it struck her: "Suppose we say that Tanili is Russian; she's defected, or is a double agent; she'd have to be taken in, perhaps not publicly acknowledged, but she'd be granted access to all treatments Nasa offers."

"Or she'd be tortured," Adam said. "Homeland Security and every other agency might get involved."

"Do you have a better plan?" Nori asked.

Adam had no plan. The sense of power was sufficient. He didn't have to do more. Seeking authority would be to lose it. It came with obligations he didn't want. Freedoms would shrink, not expand, for him at least. Life was fine as it was, with little denied. Speeding up the future could end him in court, with double fines and absurd community service to the isolated. "Utopias don't work beyond a decade. In seclusion, imbalance sets in. Leaders become deluded, if not self-defeating. No, we are not creating a political party. A web, a network, yes. We can watch people crawl through it, or turn on the glue, for dessert.

Being an overlay, a template, the crust of the pie, that's enough."

"Ambivalence does not a good husband make," Nori said.

"Your apples are tasty, for sure, but how many can I eat?"

"Can we spend the rest of the day in bed?"

And so they did for much of the week. At the end of the month, Tanili, Cran, and Celestina returned, and all was normal at the house again. Relatively. From Switzerland Tanili bought back the bean in an ice pack. Cran now sported a limp. Of course Celestina's sparkle and charm increased. "What happened?" she asked Cran.

"I was threatened, beaten, and dumped in despair that I'd not recover. I didn't get inside. My attackers weren't the 6. These were too quick and efficient, and didn't hide their faces. The local hospital called the police. I couldn't identify anyone in the mug books. The sketch artist was good, but not good enough. No one left their fingerprints on me. These goons were quite professional. Maybe they were hired."

"Did they say anything?"

"'Go home. Next time you won't be able to.'"

Less than 4 weeks later, the general found Wildcat in his backyard, in far worse shape than Cran. Tanili had the strange sense that Wildcat had done the injury to himself.

AND YET HE TOO was damaged internally, much like Jared, with systemic breakdown, loss of natural defenses, and ill health. It was obvious in his paleness, thinning, anxiety, and confusion. He was doubly hurt on being attacked.

The general and Tanili stood over Wildcat, not sure what to do with him. They couldn't help him. No one could, it seemed. It might be best to bury him where he was. The general lifted Wildcat and carried him to the street. Wildcat protested, fully awake now. "I take care of myself!" he shouted.

"Not on my watch," the general said. "Die somewhere else."

"I'm the only one who can help you," Wildcat said.

"I'll have you hanging you by your bowtie before I believe you," the general said.

"Then you'll never know the truth," Wildcat said. "Take me inside and I'll tell you."

Anticipating Wildcat to confess to twisted lies, Tanili still nodded to the general to comply.

In the wood shop, Tanili tied Wildcat down on the table saw.

"He's your prisoner. Don't abuse him," the general said.

"I've taken your implant out of me. I don't hurt when you hurt. I don't hear you thinking in your own voice now, but I know lies without listening. Speak up! Give it a try," Tanili said.

"I won't apologize," Wildcat said, "because I don't possess the whole truth, but Futura decided to eliminate us one by one. Jared went first. He's gone. It's my turn now. She's purging the ranks and bingeing on new experiments. She put fish genes into Jared and a lizard's into me. I don't know that for sure, I just suspect. She hired police to complete the job. They followed me here. I didn't lead them to you. Cran already did."

"Why? Why did you come here?"

"You're the only one who can save me, and the others. The gene-broth worked on you. You can lend me some of your blood, and brains. Do I have to beg? Can I just ask?"

"I don't know which part of that weave is truth and which lies," Tanili said.

"It's all a lie!" Wildcat shouted abruptly. "I came to see you die. I'll live."

Tanili slapped at his face. She saw visions, of snow mountains on a beach and Wildcat leading her to them. Suddenly the rock star, he climb spiral stairs to his hospital room, humming Beethoven melodies, followed by loud sloppy pop.

Tanili knew, she'd never get the full truth from him. He didn't have it.

"Perversity kills," she said, "but truth won't help you now either. You're dead. I can speed up the process. You want that?"

"I know your secret, why you survived," Wildcat said. "Help me with your blood, and I'll tell you. I stole Futura's notes."

Tanili tightened the table belts. "Listen carefully," she said, "These tools are new, sharp, the best of kind, and want to be used." She brought out a carcass saw, a dead blow mallet, a center punch, an electric branding iron, and milk paint to the table. "We can put you on a lathe and, with a turning chisel, make you into a spindle, then cover you with coconut oil, lemon juice and wax to hold in the bleeding. With camera help we might make you into a billboard, larger than life, but dead, with your wells and refineries drained, and your slogans peeling. Don't think we won't?"

Her eerie maniacal focus, her knowing soft tone frightened Wildcat to his core. She wouldn't back away from torture. But he'd nothing more to promise or give. He couldn't remember the contents of Futura's notes, and with every moment was less sure of where he'd hid them.

"Your hearse will be a thousand billboards coast to coast," Tanili said, "You betrayed the forest, you presumed about me, you trusted your club, but pirated its mission. You are extinct."

Wildcat didn't respond. Tanili smashed his ankles with the leaded rubber mallet. The general was sure she'd do all she said, but he didn't stop her. Tanili paused. More than anything she wanted to drill a hole in Wildcat's head, to do to him what had been done to her. She put a speed drill to his skull. "Wait!" he shouted, "I just remembered. My final will is in my grandfather's urn in the attic. Please let my wife know. And please understand, everything I did was for you and her."

Having seen enough torture, the general shot Wildcat in the drill hole. Gone was his misery. The copper bullet blew out the other side of his skull.

"I'll help you clean this up," Tanili said, as if relieved.

"What am I missing? What happened between you two? Do I want to know?" the general asked.

"It's better if you don't."

The general stared at her in growing awe. A fearless leader, Tanili had better creds than a reluctant sluggard like Adam.

"You tell us what you want," the general said, "but my voice lays down the law for strategy and tactics. Agreed? We punish slackers too."

Tanili ignored him and covered Wildcat with milk paint for its uneven antique look. He became a sculpture. The center piece for a modern ballet, she thought. Or maybe a Madison Avenue gallery. "He Didn't Feel My Pain" made a good title.

She asked the general to build a custom wood coffin to ship to Nebraska. Properly packed in dry ice, identified as "Personal Effects", Wildcat might surprise Futura coldly.

"We should be shipping him to Mexico to sell his organs there," the general said regretfully.

"Bad, the recipient would die too, thanks to the donor."

Tanili and the general didn't relate events to Nori or Adam, who were absorbed drinking a beer without borders, Stubborn Mule. "Enough foam and fluff!" the general said, "Tanili is our new leader, even if she won't consent."

"She'd make a good truing tool, taking the hills and valleys out of your grinding wheel," Adam answered.

"She'd dress you all down nicely," Nori added, laughing.

Celestina popped out of the kitchen. "The dough's resting

for the blind baking," she said. "Who's going to make bowls from the new manzanita burls that Redbud sent?"

"What're you 3 playing at?" the general asked.

"We could hear the wood screaming from here," Adam said. "Was that your wife, or the wood not letting go of its life? Not telling? Then let's talk about the flavor here, malting the hops the Maryland way. Sit down, have a pale ale. It's not time to be serious, yet."

"I had a showdown with the President yesterday. I didn't win, but he lost," said the general.

"Adam will wear your stars before I do," Tanili replied. "Let him. His sense of things comes from experience that I don't have. Yes, I'll grow into my brain soon enough, I hope, if you all can wait."

THE SPECTROGRAPHIC scans from the genetic samples growing on the cube-sat came back regularly. Nothing was revealed, but then, no one in the clan knew what they were looking for or how to interpret the data in any case.

Tanili's brain scans were a different matter. Adam and Nori stitched them together, using Nasa software, as if they were the grid of a galaxy. The swirls and clouds of color fascinated Tanili also. The bright centers were constant, whatever she was doing. Thoughts took shape only in emissions, it seemed; these could be read by Tanili at least. More and more, she knew what she was thinking, before the thought.

The scans simply confused Celestina. "How does this affect global warming?" she asked.

"Earth as a brain can't think for itself. The more we think for it, the worse off we get," Tanili said. "What's your plan?"

"I'm here for fun. I haven't had enough. What's yours?"

"I came to Washington to be allowed to exist, or get a planet of my own. Not realistic of me, I know that now, but hiding in a community in hiding beats all," Tanili said.

"I'm running a safe house?" Nori asked, uncertainly.

"That's bad. We're doomed. I won't realize my biological destiny," Celestina said.

"I can't have children," Nori said. Adam wasn't surprised.

"Your doctor told me too," he said. "My search for an heir is getting me nowhere. Would that I could create my own descendants, or adopt Tanili, perhaps. The goal is still to begin things here, then encourage them everywhere. A fountain of energy, a mountain of youth, a family of friends."

"I've stepped up, so, so don't I count?" Celestina asked.

"Always," Adam said, smiling at his hissing sister-in-law.

"But I'm the most recently born," said Tanili.

"And the most dangerous," Nori said. "We need a safe house for you across the ocean, on the other side of the planet."

"My inheritance is invisible," Adam mused. "My dad knew nothing, because he didn't want to. I made up for that. Cran's father is a master because he tests himself constantly. He's sharper now that his warped personality doesn't get in the way. Indifference, that's the ticket to brains."

"Which brain?" Tanili asked.

"The ones we're given."

"I'd share mine if you'll let me, but if you want me to go somewhere else, I will," Tanili offered.

"No. We're happy you're here," Nori said, "but we need a trap door, straight through, to Japan, maybe."

"Kyoto, Iwakuni, Hokkaido sound good to me," Adam said.

"Who do we know?" Celestina asked.

Tanili thought about where she didn't want to go: to the Sierras, India, and Patagonia.

Within days Tanili learned the rudiments of Japanese. With tapes, she could speak it within a week. "I can go ahead, and set up," she said. "What am I trying to set up?"

"Influence in Asia," Adam said, "Hand out my 1ACROSS cards. Solicit executive portraits. Yes, we fine-tune global identities as visual consultants. We map the national mind, facilitate communication world-wide. We're designers crafting the message."

"Can you believe him?" Nori asked.

"Cran and I and the general will stake you," Adam went on to Tanili. "We're a solutions company. Really! We don't need money. We love the challenge. The reward is the back door."

"Your mind is a maze you never get lost in," Tanili said, "How? Why? Have you just never grown up?"

"One brain can have 12 tracks, or 100. I'm a trainyard, but you'll own your sponsors in time, and their signal-house."

Tanili flew to the West Coast, en route to Japan. On landing in San Francisco, the stewardess, with a U.S. flag tie, shouted, "All rise!"

IWAKUNI IS ONLY a short ride to Hiroshima. With citizenship and the general's authority, Tanili slept overnight in officers' quarters. The Japanese guarding the base saluted her as she bicycled out. She bought a dragon-decorated jacket at her 1st stop, with Adam in mind. At the railroad crossing, a woman with a megaphone shouted orders to the dozen men cleaning the track. Tanili pedalled on, over the arching Samurai bridge, with tourists clinging to its rails. Above her, American Marine jets raced toward China, for practice, then turned back. At last Tanili arrived at the rebuilt city, in time to watch the glass-domed sightseeing boats light up at dusk.

The next morning she rode the bullet train to Kyoto. The lacquered grace of the waiters left a trace in her thoughts. She was nearing her goal. A neat precise little man from the government met her for an expensive hotel lunch. "Your presence honors us," he said, bowing deeply.

"And I am honored to be in your company," Tanili said. "The Minister of Culture must have many obligations beyond his old friends. Did the general tell you of my purpose?"

"He said you were a layered pearl who I should meditate on, to find the future. I asked if you were natural or cultured. He said you were both."

"Ah so, I already have 2 husbands. Now I wish a prince."

"Not a king?"

"No, I must grow. I will with your help."

"It shall be done," the Minister said, and bowing deeply, left her alone.

The flow in the hotel lobby intrigued her. She stood apart, as if on a river bank. Fish jumped past. The staff flew. Tanili floated up to the tree tops on the mezzanine, then drifted down.

She left the next day for Hokkaido. Three boys scratched curses in her rental car. Their mother cried. Fishing boats stranded by the tide keeled over. A black train powered through the freezing bleakness. Tanili flew back to Kyoto.

"We are committed," the Minister said.

"As we are to you," Tanili said. "Feel free to engage us, in pleasure and leisure and struggle."

The general was waiting by his phone for her judgment. It was certain: "The minister's loyalty and trust will provide us what's needed. Wee have allies."

Suddenly Tanili realized, she could perceive more deeply, clearly, and surely than ever before. Though war was never spoken, she understood, it was at the core of all.

More trips were ore trips with mines and gifts pre-arranged. Tanili's presence sealed the commitment. The ministers felt ordained, as if in a lordly attendance. "Life is good. Living is better. Being your breath is best," Tanili texted Adam.

Like the Gingko tree she felt free of disease. She'd survived the thorium bean. It was gone from her spine for good.

"Religion isn't allowed. Keep a spirit without stone. You've no need to atone," Adam texted back.

Junior generals knew how to lead after all, Tanili thought.

On return to Washington, she questioned Nori about the unity of competing symmetries. Nori didn't have a Nasa answer. Tanili went back to her day to day.

"The Russians need our attention too," Adam said. "Abroad, it's all sick tricks without voodoo. Synthetic DNA offers 50 IQ gene pools. Otherwise, Russia is succeeding where we need them to fail, and failing where we plan to pirate their success."

"I heard in Japan, the general is testing a next-gen assault rifle on our Russian peers," Tanili said. "He thinks I can aim and fire without sights or a trigger, without touch or wires, by mindfulness somehow, but he wants live ammo on a real battlefield, not a simulation. No, I'm not off to Ukraine or Chechnya. If I'm to be kidnapped let it happen here."

Weeks later Tanili agreed to the general's game: meeting the Russians at Union Station in DC and tracking their aspirations.

"Test-tube steaks for test-tube brains does not a human

make," Adam said. "The Russians will have no regard for you, but give them a challenge that mocks their ability and they'll rise to your height. They'll be surly and insular also, at first."

"We want to know what they know," the general said. "We're not looking for allies."

"I can scan them for nervous tics and tells, but what good is that? Maybe I can anticipate them as well, but then what?"

"Listen for White Swans, jets in Russia, codenamed Black-jacks by Nato. They're on their way to Venezuela."

Tanili was curious. Adam encouraged her quest. The general only wanted specifics.

Waiting for Tanili in an open bar, Russian diplomats sat with their backs to the wall. Officially they were consular officers, but these were obvious security, grim, blunt, and determined.

Tanili altered her tact. "I got where I am by rubbing noses till it hurt," she said, "I've a slush fund for trips. You may join me in the Caribbean, where the molé mayonnaise is excellent."

"You have big head for dancer," the stocky blond Russian said, "Is that cover story?"

"Once upon a time I had another life. I hurt people," Tanili said, "Now I watch words dance. What would you like to hear?"

"Informations. Apologies for sanctions. Permissions to pass your sky."

"I have friends of friends with friends, I'm not at the center of anything, but I can deliver messages. I was a criminal too once. You can trust me."

"You admit to crime, so we confess. Good strategy. Win vodka. You come with us. We show you truth."

"I'm not who you think I am."

"We think nothing, just good time. Come, now!"

He grabbed her wrist. She waved to a nasty-looking cop watching her. He approached the table. "These men want to know how to get to the White House from here. Show them the way to Leavenworth instead, and I owe you," Tanili said, and left.

SHE WANTED TO BLAME the general for sending her on a fool's errand, but bigger fools abound.

A stranger singled her out of the crowd as she stepped onto the street. "You're responsible!" he screamed at Tanili. "Why don't you respond? Where's your conscience? You have to share with those less —"

"Blow away, butch. Go! Do I look like a victim?"

The stranger went on a tear, stopping with his final spear: "How can you wear African beads, when you're —?"

"They're coffee beans. Flutter off, you bird-bath-brain."

"All the worse. You're appropriated my life."

"And you my language, dim-witless."

"I earned it, I paid for it. The only way you can be proud is by sharing my pride."

"You're contradicting yourself. Anyway, your only asset is my fear quotient, which is zero. Now step away."

Instead the stranger menacingly moved toward her. The same nasty-looking cop stepped inbetween and, with a round-house elbow to the chin, dropped the stranger to his knees. Tanili left at her leisure.

The world was no saner at home. Normally no one in the clan watched broadcast news or knelt on its pews, but fresh revelations belied common belief. Harvard's endowment was investment-buying California water rights. And Warren Buffett, on pledging most of his money to charity, wanted full control of Nevada electricity. Supposedly, he'd have more to give back. Unusually cross-wired and hypocritical, the news amused.

"All roads here lead backward," Tanili said, "A dozen brains won't clear the air. We need our morons to take the 1st bullets."

"And when the enemy runs out of ammo?" Adam asked.

"There'll always be more," Nori said. "We aren't alone in the universe."

CELESTINA FAT-CHECKED herself every morning, pinching her waist to measure the loose flesh, folded. The right answer: under an inch. She'd been entering contest calls also: the next generation condom award especially had potential. Yet, the odd reality that one side of her body was aging quicker than the other concerned her more, as she was only 28. She wanted an easy solution, but messing with your own DNA outside a medical office was less than legal, which might still be okay, if someone else took the fall, if failure was evident.

Nori stayed home. Without a budget, the government shut down, it was a crime to work, literally. She left her tablet in her Nasa office and brought home her potted plants: the coffee tree from Peru, the mango palm from Ecuador.

Elsewhere, Turkey bombed the Kurds, and Taliban struck Kabul, but it was of little consequence to the rest of the world.

Tanili no longer traveled. France, past and present, lost its appeal. The slogan, 'DeGaulle was tall and that's about all' led to Paris riots about little people. Germany went from leading world slaughter to outlawing comedy, big time in fact, by defining all humorous insinuations as hate speech. The CIA travel advisory for Mali said, make sure your will is in order, and you have no unfinished business at home, for starters. Clearly, no incentive to travel there.

Cran reported in from San Francisco: "The Mission street festival drumming gave me an ear ache."

"No wonder the Spanish are stupid, they can't hear themselves think," Tanili said.

"Does having a 4th brain intensify your base prejudices?" Cran asked.

"You're right, I'm judgemental when I'm vulnerable. It's push-back. I'm assaulted wherever I go, mentally."

With trips postponed or permanently canceled, she found threats at home more pressing. They hinted everywhere. Her plastic surgeon husband, kidnappers from foreign powers, the Nebraska club, random street aggression, and odd political posturing hinted openly that she'd be forever in jeopardy.

"Constructive paranoia has its place," Adam said.

The general had easy answers: sophisticated weaponry. His Scottish ancestors went back more than a millenia to battle bishops who led their own troops and prolonged the Middle Ages for 500 years before being over-run by Vikings. In time the family name changed from Blood Axe to Blunt, but the sons lapsed into being heathens as weapons grew invisible. Yet, the general still believed first, steel sharpens steel, in battle.

His calm forward focus was always evident. In her way Tanili caught up with him though. "Your confidence used to hang by a thread, instead of float in an envelope. Now, it's moved on to aggressive," Adam said to her.

"It's not a choice," she answered. "My thoughts write themselves in code now, and my eyes roll up every scene like a scroll. I worry about running out of room."

"Life is the sum of all possibilities," Adam said. "Of course, only the rich and the conoscenti can be everywhere at once."

"A plain electron can play the same game," Nori teased.

"In theory. In verse. In total confusion. It can't know where it is."

"Should we eat out tonight? I found a new menu in town with 3-D printed food, from beetroot and cardamom mostly. The deli there is working on meat without animals, growing stem cells from the unborn into juicy burgers. I want to check it out for the space station," Nori said. "Let's go taste it."

"No. Enzymes follow instructions," Adam said, "I do not."

"C'mon, you're my cut man. I've got to fight in this ring."

"In time," Adam said, "In thermoplastic exuberance."

"A real fight," Nori said. "Against a plasma rifle, a vomit gun, an LED incapacitator, or just sharp knuckles."

"It's your scuffle. I'll hold the fort."

"We're a tag team. Engagement rules are strictly enforced."

But a visit to the restaurant was not to be. Jared Agh, with a hospital name-tag, and Patagonia showed up at the front door. Tanili answered it. "I thought you were dead," she said to Jared.

"I feel like it," he said.

"I'm trying to save him, but he's a hard cure," Patagonia said.

"You'd better go," Tanili said, "He will die here, otherwise."

"India wants him dead as a man, and Futura too. She already has what she wants from him, his seeds and sperm. I need your brain to decipher her notes. Wildcat stole them for me. They're pictograms, or complex wiring diagrams for electronic implants. I made them for her in the first place, and she annotated them. You have the key code to her mind. The vanilla bean in your spine has her DNA and it talks to you. Jared's gone wrong. You can right him. Her chemical symbols aren't yet accepted. By the time they are, it'll be too late for Jared. And me."

"Does one choice preclude the other?"

"That's up to you."

"I destroyed the vanilla bean, or I'd have known you were coming. Terrible thing I did, isn't it? With the bean talking to me incessantly, I was afraid to even nap, that I'd miss something, that I'd die in my sleep under instruction from the doctor. No, the bean terrified me. It began to think for itself. It webbed the 6 of you into a single mind, trying to control me, and using me to control you. I wished you all ill."

"You killed us!"

"If you're not dead yet, there's no reason you will be."

"You made us grotesque!"

"I wish I'd known that I could. Sorry about that. Please, go now. My neighbor —"

The general came up the path. His underarm bulge, meant to warn people off, was clearly effective. Patagonia dragged Jared to the Lexus at the curb and was gone in seconds.

"I came to invite you to fight night. My wife and I have at it weekly. She may be a head taller than me and drive a badder Harley, but I fixed that conflict when I married her."

"Do you mind if we pass?" Tanili said. "I've had a horrible shock, just now."

"Me?"

"No, the people who left without introducing themselves."

"Should I know them?"

"It would be the biggest mistake of your life," Tanili said and went back inside, to check on the bean. She hadn't destroyed it. The iced, lead foil case was still tightly wrapped. The next day she had a sub-zero refrigerator and a back-up generator installed in the basement lab. The bean might be her joy stick and ace in the hole yet, if she kept it alive and frozen well.

Especially with the consecutive AGU and AAAS meetings ahead: 60,000 scientists coming to DC to share their research and re-weave the global agenda. What was it worth to examine her and the bean? How many would kill for her?

Then again, why would she need them to?

Futura and dozens of others could prep, if he wanted to, a recellularized cardiac scaffold for Jared to live to full life. Magic bullets for zombies, on the other hand, were video candy that left her hungry. Not the concern of the initiated. But didn't we eat Neanderthal also?

Why Tanili had survived when others didn't was a more pressing question to her. Perhaps she wasn't alone. Maybe there were cities of extra-sentient life in the making.

If electricity in one brain shaped the other, gave it pocket membranes and paths to communicate, based on self-catalytic re-action, then — Anything is possible. Clouds blow clear over time, or shower down on us.

Judgment is irrelevant. Morality preserves authority, simple as that. Competition denies it.

Tanili's thoughts spiraled through her and escaped into the night.

ADAM AND CRAN were out of their league in their pursuit of big science. They created a cloud chamber, hoping to measure the radiation of Tanili's brain, in effect, to watch its sparks fly. They practiced using americium from old smoke detectors, but when it came to surrounding her large head with super-cooled, super-saturated alcohol, they nearly froze her to death. To read her brain, they needed an alphabet or at least a unit of measurement, that translated into capabilities. They had nothing but a few laughs at their own ineptitude.

"Should brain drown, wear a mermaid crown, should brain freeze, an end to sneezes," Adam said, giggling.

Tanili was aware though that the shape of her head was changing. Online research revealed no precedents. Historically, the invention of fire and farming allowed for rapid increases in brain size. In theory, deep data and artificial intelligence just might do the same, creating very real over-sized intelligence, or maybe just robots, and an end to wonder.

With access provided by Nori, Tanili, Adam and Cran spent weeks studying at the Smithsonian and the Library of Congress. In the curator's quarters, they sorted through endless boxes of artifacts that might never see display. Collectively the domed buildings were a researcher's dream: brains themselves housing all human thought, expressed and evolving. A very real sense of discovery exhilarated the 3, who came away informed with potential if not specific answers. If the truth was everything, it took lifetimes to realize this. The curators indeed gave their lives to cataloguing every last bone, pen point and alphabet.

Yet, official Washington wasn't a cradle of new living forms. Still, the eco-police were out in force: nuts, seeds, and sprouts, trying to crush all exuberance: "What's the climate footprint of your lipstick?" one asked Tanili. "Or your brain-weight and what's in it? Girl, you've got a big head."

In reaction, Tanili realized her natural prima donna role:

she'd been reborn in a club, was adopted by a clan, and now had a cult forming around her, not seeking to isolate itself in remote jungles. No dues or contributions required, only shared unique brainwaves, please. Why shouldn't it be her century to lead?

Tanili winced at her own vanity. She understood the failings of pride, how it blind-sided many a ballerina, on stage and off. She was prepared to suffer, as she knew she would. To her the universal here was too specific. The radioactive thorium, the unknowns of her creation, of her guarded existence, and her ongoing evolution were unmapped, but still a life-time cross-continental trip, with only grit to guide her in survival.

She began to see herself grow. Perfectly formed models of everything existed in her mind already, symmetries in variation, fractured shadows, impossible configurations, contortions in a vacuum, fluctuating boundary energies, all expanding and shrinking at once, trapped at absolute zero, or pressurized, volatile, uncontained. The shaping and reshaping didn't stop. Shadows fought with their subjects, sides of an object competed with each other, sparks flying in all directions, like a fuse ever-burning. Everything classic was fixed; nothing quantum was set. All states of being existed at once, and Tanili, more aware of them than ever, was unable to contain them. Her genes ordered new nerve cells now and insulated them: basal ganglia in a myelin sheath, but somehow different. Extra-ordinary thoughts gripped her. Only life as a squid could save her. Blots and dots and clouds of purple ink swirled behind her eyes in endless wild surprise and wonder.

Yet, she might as well have been a mushroom, rooted to the spot, self-multiplying in confusion.

Under-the-table calm possessed her. Only Adam seemed to understand: "Beyond the tallest woods is the wild ocean, but at my feet a fungus swells slowly," he said.

"I met 3 eco-trolls today who still live with their mothers," Tanili answered.

A PhD PSYCHIATRIST came to the house, to analyze Tanili non-invasively. That she'd been a dancer was clear in her graceful stride; expert plastic surgery was also evident in the sharpness of her features; quick responses revealed confidence and agility, but the normal/abnormal span of interests was wholly missing.

"What's your favorite toy? What about hobbies?"

"You're Nori's bad idea? She didn't warn me."

"What about your favorite food? Or actor?"

"You want pop culture to define me?"

"I'm trying to find where you best fit in the world."

"Are you a job counselor also?"

"You don't want to be a burden to society, do you? You must have some talent."

"Less than you, I assume, that you presume."

"I know all about me. My job is to define you."

"And my whole point is not to let you. I can be an echo, an international organizer, a waitress, a slouch. I was for starters."

"Are you qualified to be?"

"Did Nori hire you out of the parking lot at Home Depot?"

"What do you have against Mexicans?"

"You look Filipino to me."

"Same thing, isn't it, since we all look alike."

"As I look identical to your category chart."

"Being hostile won't get you a job."

"If I slit your throat, I'd create 10 jobs for other people."

"You should go to therapy."

"And graduate with a degree in Freudian toilets?"

"I can see you don't take me seriously."

"I've no reason. But you've given me an idea, to create a test that's right for me."

She borrowed radio-telescope audios of cosmic rays, to see what patterns she could find. "These were reviewed," Nori said. "They showed no signal sense, just static."

Tanili identified subtle, complex surges. "Guess what? I'm a self-cancelling wave at heart, a wonky navigator," she beamed, and charted the gravitational tensions. "Really I'd prefer to hear the howling swirl of Nebraska winds, to predict tornadoes if not hurricanes. Force categories are easy, for a chaser. Curiously, to be fair, I seem to've acquired perfect pitch, but that doesn't make me a singer."

The broken harmonies that Tanili caught opened up new possibilities. She was as likely as an algorithm to identify coded alien transmissions. She toyed with the idea of a Nasa job she could do at home, with earphones, anonymously, then declined Nori's offer. But it was clear to everyone in the clan, Tanili was absorbing each member's brain without intending to. And now she knew it.

She also discovered, her brain had its own sense of sound. Its fundamental wasn't a single frequency but a cord, and the harmonics multiplied sharply, to form a web of nearly infinite nodes, that trapped previously unrecognized prime patterns, to no obvious survival purpose.

She was clearly over her head now and searched for a mute button till she found one in deeper layers of sleep.

THE OTHER CLANS Tanili connected with, on her travels for Adam and the general, weren't as appealing to her. They were mind-worms, alive to the bird-brains around them, from a distance. She thought of herself protectively, as a red-breasted falcon now, ravenous, out-pacing every winged species.

She wanted to give up Earth entirely, but the clans, as a league, held her, gave her tentacles and advantage.

Adam was still their nominal leader, not leading.

Tanili was tempted, as if she'd just woken up to her own adolescence, to find herself smarter, more energetic, disciplined and capable than anyone else she'd ever met.

Dominating with her body, having been a dancer, was easy. Having to do so with her mind caused panic attacks, full with insecurity and a sense of doom. Her knowledge was intuitive, borrowed, and unable to sustain itself or expand on a given path. Dance was so much simpler; it required repetition, muscle memory, timing, and little more.

Futura had somehow lucked into the right choices, having worked in the field so long. Her genetic alphabet wasn't a tower of Babel, or crippling, but Tanili had a long way to travel, to master its language, on its grid of incremental steps.

She needed crutches. Maybe it was time to grab control of Cran. Celestina was a straw weight. She drew the dragon-flies, but her lotions and potions were the finest. She worked for an Israeli company that made distinctive colors, flavors, and fra-grances for the world's top luxury brands. Celestina, with Adam's help, created the company slogan: "The brains behind the blessing, a hydration of forever."

Tanili spent a week trying out samples. Her skin became silken and electric. Cran thrilled to her accidental touch, as she brushed against his arm. He wanted to seize her and hold on, as if she was what life was meant to be. Instead he offered to take her to a Violet Headmess concert on the rave scene, with free tickets provided by Celestina. Tanili declined. Celestina indifferently suggested born-beautiful.com for a newer ocean of options. Her motives seemed uncertain, but it was clear that Washington had many more-golden-handcuffs, if that's what a woman wanted. Definitely Celestina had her own agenda, and Cran had lost his value for it.

Tanili took her time. She had to. Cran traveled to the West Coast regularly. Like Tanili, he had his own space at the clan encampment. The garden offered the best private meeting place thanks to the density of the tall trees, but the dining room's communal mood seemed more suggestive. Contact in a crowd was amplified.

Nori's central dish that evening was silky tofu soup, still boiling in a cast iron bowl, with rice and pickled radish on the side. Nori broke a raw egg into her portion and quickly stirred an egg drop layer.

"Poor David, my ex-husband," Tanili said, in the direction of Cran. "He never got me pregnant."

At the end of the meal, she stood facing him, challenging, hoping to bring out the animal in him. Indeed, he followed quickly to the tented platform in the back woods. Wetly she waited on the down bed. The full moon above flooded over her, high-lighting her fullness.

Spent, Cran looked terrified, as if she were about to devour him, as if she was supposed to. For a moment, Tanili wondered whether she should.

Silently she returned to the house. Cran didn't follow. The brief taste of life and death in her lingered, pinning him down.

As Tanili's capabilities grew, her awareness expanded too. She had guided Cran's hands, willfully to her, as she wished, over his reluctance, but she didn't stop his fright or deny it to him. His fear resisted her, stopped her hands cold, and pushed her into the distance. Though she triggered his fear, it was less of her than of himself. She wondered what was in him, that she couldn't reach?

Yet, for the moment, it seemed true, that she could give consciousness to other life forms, to his left hand but not his right, to the fluttering leaves of a tree but not its roots, and then reverse her powers in an instant.

Perhaps, as life advances, it unlearns what it can do, and doesn't realize that it's communicating or are even able to. Maybe it lives in an integrated sensory world, photo-tropically determined again, and that's enough.

That all possibilities may exist simultaneously confused and irritated Tanili. That conscious focus alone, and nothing else, determined what happened, and which tunnel we entered was by its nature limiting. She wanted a thousand more brains.

She wanted to talk to Adam, the playful thinker, not Cran, the smart doer, who didn't understand himself. That was clear now, but Adam denied her. "You're just an apple, with a new snake inside," he said. "Own the truth. You've the luck of the pagan Picts, or the 15 tribes of Wales: none at all," he added.

"Think queen bee," Tanili countered.

Adam smiled. "Would that it were so," he said, "but human drones don't know their place, have purpose now, and won't be programmed."

The back and forth continued. The linear prevailed, in zigzag fashion, and then it didn't. Nori suggested a small house community on the road to Ojo Sarco, east of the Rio Grande, for Tanili's hive. Celestina added a shaman whose medicine bag offered conduits to other worlds, living hallucinations, no minds needed. Adam vetoed the mystical, as such, insisting that Tanili's future be contained within Nasa science.

Tanili returned to her platform tent, and found Cran still sprawled on the bed. She curled with him and slept till dawn, when she woke from a dream, playing a bagpipe so intensely that she'd have gone on naturally, if her fingers held the actual keys.

This had happened before, differently. She'd dreamed of needing a new red blouse for an imaginary event and rushed to the store on waking, before realizing she'd deceived herself.

Now, at dusk, panic prevailed. Her shallow breath paused, stopped, painfully started again. She willed herself to breathe slowly. Sweating heat, her chest felt chilled. She coughed and kept coughing till her throat was raw. She discovered then that the crippling panic increased as her lungs shrank, but that she could cause them to expand on intake, by thinking for them. Within minutes she was comfortable again.

She sought out Nori's doctor, who gave her 4 maximum dose prescriptions. Adam cut the pills in quarters for her. Definitely medicine was easier than thinking through a cure, when no one was sure of the disease.

The royal jelly seemed unaffected though.

Cran came to Tanili every night for 3 weeks before flying back to San Francisco. If California remained the bridge to nowhere, riches still collected at its feet.

MORE AND MORE, Tanili puzzles over herself. She wants guides that don't exist. Sharing should be simple and direct, but never is. Threats come in many forms, unexpected or unknown.

When dangers and desires go hand in hand though, love handles offer a poor grip, best not to depend on.

Cran had no rules. Only discovery excited him. Sex didn't break the barriers between them.

Indeed, Cran told Tanili that he had 100 patent inspectors always floating in his head. The men wore black tuxedos, and their ebony skiffs aligned to form a diamond shape, but none closed the distance to the shore at night, unless he signaled to them all.

Nori, as acting division director of late, had to navigate her share of Inspector Generals at Nasa. Lawyers all, they reported every conflict of interest to Congress. Tanili was only a rumor to them.

To Adam, Tanili was a toy, novel, foreign, and as complex in flavor as rooibos tea. She could out-think him, but she didn't know how to fully. He was thoroughly incomprehensible to her. His mind roller-coastered at speed, crashed, reversed, and laughed at his own injury.

Yet, Tanili knew that the clan, excluding Celestina perhaps, was perfect for her. They wanted nothing from her but the interplay. They knew that she'd received a guinea pig fee, but didn't care to request a share. As Adam liked to say, "Money's okay, but it's not worth working for."

With her lotions and potions, Celestina thought differently, sensually, with a depth of seductive detail that gave her claim to the wave on the dollar sign.

The general, with his impulse to violence, fed Tanili's more primitive side.

On the surface the clan seemed content, yet worry knit it together also. News of Tanili had traveled far: Saudis set out to compete with the Chinese for her. Nasa firewalls protected the clan's household connections, thanks to Nori. It also helped that Adam banned mass media and social apps from the house.

The Russians meanwhile tried direct chemical intrusion. The Chinese offered flattery and free trips to Bejing, then a speaking fee at a Chinese University.

Adam isolated himself to coordinate the counter-attacks. He found he was overwhelmed, panicked, dealing with hydra-headed monsters. He could tie them in knots, burn them to the ground, or use the general's arsenal against them, but every snake of evil grew radioactive in turn, or morphed redundantly, yet none pierced or poisoned his defenses.

Morning rounds for Adam began with unloading and re-loading wallet and pen guns, .50 caliber silenced sniper rifles, and checking stun grenades and explosive dye packets.

The electronic level only required a current check, to insure that deafening pain and electrocution mats actively awaited intruders. Fort Defiance, engraved on a small brass plaque, warned off strangers, but the unwary were in for a fatal shock.

More subtle were the disruptive brain signals to confuse strangers and distort their reality. Self-cancelling samples of the clan minds, sent simultaneously, based on their space research allowed the clan to safely escape intruders and hackers. Cran had worked out the details. Quiet rooms were lined with lead.

Even in plain sight, the clan was shielded.

Adam let out false information to misdirect the impatient toward the White House. He also released the *Enz Report*. It speculated on the political parties of the future, already growing like grass in suburbia: The Gamers versus Shadow Scientizers would replace the existing battle-players, the report predicted. Meanwhile, good luck with sightings in the tidal basin. It's filling up.

"What's my future going to be, ultimately?" Tanili asked.

"To trap more fish in our defenses," Adam said. "You and the general are good at pouncing. The encampment is a feeding pond. The pollen drift comes on its own too. You only have to wait without fear of the consequences."

"The closer to the bone, the sweeter the meat, yes, but you know that won't last."

"Welcome to the human race then. Enjoy your victims."

"Predict my future please, the one I've chosen."

"You'll die to be reborn. I don't know the details."

"That's scary, horrible. Please, will I achieve my destiny?"

Adam hesitated. Friends had given him a mountain top in New Mexico to meditate on, but he had no plan to retreat.

Nor did he answer her then. Instead, he wrote a book for her, *The Abattoir of Wonder*, in which all her fears came true: she lost her sense of wonder before her life ended. Jaded, she died at 31, otherwise unsung. Nasa never claimed her. A self-fulfilling prophesy, she inherited her only future.

A boy and a girl survived her, raised by Nori, with Adam and Cran's help.

CPSIA information can be obtained
at www.ICGtesting.com
Printed in the USA
FSHW011344200319
56482FS